Alex

MW00879140

Alex and the iMutts

By: Robert Healy

Alex and the iMutts

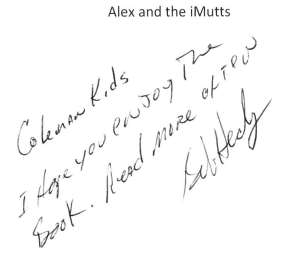

Coleman Kids
I Hope you enjoy the
Book. Read more often
Ed Healy

DEDICATED TO:
AJ, DANA ROSE, JACK, LYNDSAY-PAIGE,
MARY, YSABEL AND WILLIAM

ACKNOWLEDGMENTS:
A special thanks to all those that encouraged me through this process, particularly: My wife, Dana, my sister-in-law Bonnie Buck, my daughter, Jennifer, daughter-in-law Cathy, her Mum Frances Jamieson, Tara McDaniel and my writing coach Andrea Alban.

Alex and the iMutts

1. The Cannonball

Alex Logan made a perfect jackknife dive off the low board at the deep end of the school pool. He kicked his legs and headed up toward the surface. The water above him exploded and a violent blow rocked his head forward. Another blow pummeled his back and knocked the breath out of him. The force of the collision drove him down toward the bottom of the pool. Alex was dazed and fought to stay conscious as he sank deeper into the water. Alex could see light above him at the surface, but it looked far away. He struggled to move toward the surface, but he was confused and he desperately needed air. Alex fought the panic that rose in him, but finally against all logic, he inhaled.

Water filled his lungs, his arms and legs refused to move as his mind entered a dream state. He drifted in slow motion, suspended in his watery tomb. Alex floated like the snow in a Christmas globe; the kind you can shake and watch as fake snow swirls and falls slowly around Santa's sleigh and reindeer. In his dream, he saw a tunnel of light and someone waving to him. The figure silently drifted closer toward him. Time seemed suspended.

To his shock, Alex recognized the mysterious waving figure. It was his father. But his father had died some months ago, killed by a terrorist bomb at the Boston Marathon. How could his father be with him here and now? What was he trying to say? The figure moved nearer still, and Alex realized that his father was not waving for him to come closer. He was telling Alex to go back, to live. Someone or something grabbed his arm and his body moved upward. Alex glimpsed the light at the surface of the pool, but then everything went black.

Alex's spirit floated in the air, suspended above his lifeless body. He could see himself lying face down on the concrete near the pool's edge. Alex wondered how he could be hovering above his own body like this. Coach Fish kneeled over him and pumped his chest. Water spilled out of Alex's gaping mouth and spread onto the concrete. He pumped Alex's chest several more times and more water poured from his mouth. Then Coach Fish rolled Alex over and felt for a pulse that was not there. He pumped Alex's chest with both hands ... short, strong strokes, one, two, three, four. Three uniformed people arrived, pushing a wheeled stretcher. One of them bent down and breathed into Alex's gaping mouth, filling Alex's lungs with much needed air.

Another pumped his chest. Alex's floating spirit looked at his classmates, who stood frozen nearby. Most of them were horrified, their hands covered their mouths and some were sobbing ... but Bart Quisling was joking with his friends.

Pump, pump, pump ... another long breath was forced into Alex's lungs. Pump, pump, pump ... and then another breath. Alex felt himself being drawn back toward his motionless body by an irresistible force. Down, down his spirit traveled, until he lost sight of his body and his classmates. He became aware of the man pumping his chest. Alex coughed convulsively and spat out more water. He coughed again and opened his eyes slightly. Alex heard someone say, "Yes! Yes! He's coming around!"

A booming cheer of relief echoed around the pool enclosure as his classmates burst into spontaneous applause and *whoops* of celebration. Two men picked up Alex and placed him onto the wheeled gurney. They attached an oxygen mask to his face and rolled him out of the pool area to a waiting ambulance.

"Mrs. Buck! Call Mrs. Logan immediately and have her meet us at Marin General Hospital!"

"Yes, right away Mr. Fish!"

Coach Fish dismissed the class, and climbed into the ambulance to accompany Alex to the hospital. Mrs. Logan raced to meet them at the emergency room.

The ambulance siren screamed as Coach Fish looked down at Alex and said, "You are going to be all right, Alex. You gave us all a scare, but you are going to be all right."

"What happened?" Alex said in a confused, groggy voice.

"It was an accident, Alex. You were jumped on by another student when you were coming to the surface after your dive."

"Who jumped on me?" Alex asked in quiet, subdued manner.

"It was Bart Quisling, Alex. He said he didn't see you. He probably feels pretty bad about the whole thing."

Barely audible, Alex murmured, "I doubt it. Bart's a bully. He probably did it on purpose."

"You don't know that to be how it happened Alex. You shouldn't make wild accusations."

Alex's head turned wearily to one side and his eyes closed.

"Alex, just sit back and stay calm, we'll be at the hospital very soon."

The ambulance pulled into the hospital Emergency Room entrance and parked. The siren blurted a final, short *whoop*, as if exhausted by the trip. The ambulance back door flew opened and two men slid the gurney out. The gurney wheels extended down and locked into place as the men glided it forward through the open doors of the ER.

Alex's mom rushed forward, "Alex, Alex, are you all right, baby?"

Alex winced when she said "Baby." He was not a baby. He was twelve years old, and a young man. Alex fought to appear more alert than he felt.

"I'm fine mom. It's no problem, really. I'm fine. Can't we just go home now?"

"Not until they check you out, baby. They have to be sure you're okay."

"I'm fine!"

"We'll see. So how did this happen?"

"That bully Bart Quisling jumped on top of me in the pool."

"I'm sure it was an accident. Bart wouldn't do something like that on purpose."

Two physicians interrupted the conversation and pushed the gurney toward two wide self-opening doors into the examination area. *Whoosh*, the doors opened and Alex disappeared into the room. He was quickly surrounded by doctors and nurses. Alex was admitted for overnight observation and released the following day.

Alex sat quietly gazing out of the car window on the ride home with his Mom.

"Alex, what's the matter? You're so quiet."

"Tomorrow the kids at school will tease me about being totally lame for almost drowning. I'll never live this down!"

"Alex, it wasn't your fault, it was an accident. You could have died for heaven's sake! Nobody is going to tease you about that.

"You don't know these kids, Mom."

"Be cool and say, I'm fine and it's history. If you pretend it was no big deal, they will lose interest and stop teasing."

"But what if they keep teasing?"

"Just look bored and change the subject."

Alex thought about telling his Mom about how he had hovered over his own body while the rescue squad people resuscitated him, and how his Dad had appeared to him when he was under water. But then Alex thought … Maybe Mom will think I had suffered brain damage and will take me back to the hospital. No, he thought, better to keep those things to myself.

When he got home, Alex went to his room and booted up his game console. He played "Mario Smash Brothers" to blow off some steam. Alex manipulated the game controller and thought; Mom always has nice things to say about Bart, but she doesn't know him. Bart's father was Trent Quisling III, a super- successful, mega-wealthy guy, who unlike his miserable son Bart, was a very popular fellow. Alex quietly thought about how everybody in school was afraid of Bart. He wondered if swim class was a good idea as long as Bart Quisling was in the pool. Besides, humans had spent millions of years of evolution to get out of water and onto dry land. Why should we jump back into water, where there are dangerous creatures like sharks, stingrays and thugs like Bart Quisling? Bart the bully was such a total jerk, but everybody was so afraid of him.

Bart had once told Alex about his "philosophy" of fighting. Bart said that first he would wrestle, but if the other guy were better at that, he'd box. If the other guy were a better boxer, he'd start kicking and biting. If that didn't work he'd find a stick or a rock, because the fight was never over until Bart won. Alex had learned three important lessons about Bart from that conversation:

1. Don't hang around Bart Quisling.

2. Never get into a fight with Bart.

3. If you do, lose quickly.

Alex had mixed emotions of anger and fear. His mind was focused on Bart and getting payback. He was certain that Bart had purposely jumped on him, but Alex had no idea what he could do about it. Alex smoldered.

2. The iMutts

A few miles away, two young dogs sat in their cages at a secret government research laboratory. The two dogs, named Buddy and Pepper, watched a video of a dusty pick-up truck racing across rough desert terrain. The truck bounced violently and, almost overturned a few times. One of the men shouted for the driver to slow down.

He pointed toward a driveway and said, "Quick, turn left there!" The driver braked hard and made a sharp turn to the left. Rocks and clouds of dust flew as the truck skidded.

"Go straight. The house should be just ahead. There! Pull over and park."

The front door of the cabin opened. Two big dogs bounded out of the house and ran, growling and snarling, toward the truck. Two men with cowboy hats, pulled down low on their brows to hide their faces, emerged from the house with guns in their hands. They stood on the porch in dusty pants that looked two sizes too large. The trousers hovered low on their hips and seemed to be held up by some invisible power that prevented them from falling to their ankles.

The man with the a mustache growled, "Who are you? What do you want?"

The man in the passenger seat rolled his window down and said, "We're here to meet with Pedro."

"What for?"

"That's my business and Pedro's, not yours!"

"Get out of the truck slowly, with your hands in the air, where we can see them."

Both men complied, making sure not to make any sudden movements.

Pedro sauntered onto the porch. "Welcome my friends. Did you bring the money?"

"Yes. Do you have the package?"

"Of course my friends, I have what you want." But Pedro was a friend of nobody, and least of all, the two men in the truck.

The three men sat on the porch and talked for a while. Pedro went into the cottage and returned with a package, which he placed on the table. Pedro's two men watched quietly with their hands on their guns. One of the truckers went to the pickup and removed a bundle wrapped in a brown paper bag. He handed it to Pedro, who peeked inside, flipped through some bills and then passed a package wrapped in white plastic wrap to the driver of the truck. He opened a corner, examined the contents, tipped his hat and walked to the truck with his partner. The truck raced away in a cloud of dust. The video ended.

A question boomed from a speaker mounted inside of each dog's cage, "What happened in this video?"

Pepper texted a response, "Two men drove a pickup in the desert and met with Pedro and two other men at a small cabin."

Buddy added, "The pickup truck had an Arizona license plate, number TGB 237.

Pepper continued, "The truck driver gave a bag filled with money to a man named Pedro."

Buddy added, "Pedro gave the trucker a package in return and the truckers left."

The research scientist named Anna smiled and said, "Very well done, indeed! Did you capture any video of the men talking?"

Pepper texted, "Yes" and downloaded the short video of the event.

The other researcher, named Mark said, "They are making great progress, Anna, and their video-cams are working perfectly."

"Mark, I know I should be used to seeing these dogs send text messages by now, but it always amazes me how Dr. Gore's brainwave scanning technology reads their thoughts and converts them into text messages."

"Anna, sometimes I think these dogs have a better vocabulary than I do."

"No kidding, me too! But Mark how does Dr. Gore make it all work?"

"When we flash a picture or a word on their LCD monitors, a scanner reads their brainwaves. Each image the dog sees creates a unique brainwave pattern. The scanner captures each brainwave patterns and Dr. Gore's software links them to the correct English and Spanish vocabulary words stored in their embedded computers. After many repetitions, the computer can reliably understand what the dogs are thinking and converts their brainwaves into text messages."

"Mark, It all seems so logical, but magical. I wonder if this technology could work for people too?"

"Dr. Gore says his technology will replace lie detectors someday and we'll be able to know what people are thinking by monitoring their brainwaves too."

"That's a little scary, Mark. Talk about an invasion of privacy!"

Anna updated her chart and closed her notebook. Mark started up a vocabulary exercise program, and the two researchers walked out of the lab.

Neither Buddy nor Pepper liked doing the vocabulary training programs, because they were boring. The dogs listened to words spoken though a speaker mounted inside their cage. Then they pressed a blue button on one of the two smaller LCD screens inside their cage. One screen displayed the correct printed word. When they chose the right response, a tasty doggy treat was dispensed. They liked that part so they learned quickly. The scanner was busy linking their brainwave patterns to their computer dictionaries. Other times the dogs watched videos to learn how to understand and compose complete sentences and to become familiar with the world outside of the lab.

About one hour into this particular training exercise, Buddy called over to Pepper. Even the research scientists were unaware that dogs and some other animals can communicate with sounds beyond the human range of hearing. And some intelligent animals, like dogs, can also communicate using telepathy over short distances.

"Pepper, I'm bored. We know all this stuff already. I need a break!"

"Be patient Buddy, the researchers will take their afternoon break soon."

"Sometimes, Pepper, I think there has to be more to life than working on language skills inside these cages. I have an urge to go outside and run around in the grass or in the woods."

"Buddy, you should be thankful for what we have. They feed us, take care of us and we have important jobs here at the lab, learning words."

"I know that Pepper, but something is missing. I don't think we're supposed to be cooped up in cages like this all day."

"We get to go outside sometimes."

"For short walks on a leash. Remember when that nice lab tech, Sean Keegan, took us for a walk outside and how great that was. Remember how he let us off the leash to run free ... all the smells, the birds, the squirrels and running through the grass. It felt like it was where we should be ... you know, free to run. And then grouchy, Dr. Gore told Sean never to let us off-leash outside again. I tell you we're prisoners!"

"Buddy, I think you are getting carried away. I suggest you stop thinking so much. You're going to drive yourself crazy."

That was when events for Buddy and Pepper started to go totally wrong!

Robert Healy

3. Mr. Gnarly

The doors to the main research laboratory slide open with a *whoosh* followed by a soft *thud*. Two overweight uniformed security guards entered and approached one of the research scientists.

The older guard spoke first. "Dr. Gore wants us to bring two of the dogs to the main conference room for some sort of big meeting."

"Which dogs does he want?"

The guard looked at his paperwork, "Numbers AX- 275 and AX- 276."

"Buddy and Pepper. They're right over here."

The dogs raised their heads, when they heard their names, and looked over at the guards.

"Pepper, who are those guys and where are they taking us? Do you think we're going outside again?"

"I don't think so. If we were going outside, Sean Keegan would take us. No, the guard said they were taking us to a conference room for Dr. Gore's Big Meeting."

"But, why are we going to this meeting?"

"Buddy, this could be trouble. Yesterday, I heard Dr. Gore complain that his boss at The National Intelligence Agency (NIA) was unhappy about the progress of his research project."

"But what does that have to do with us?"

"**WE** are his research project, which means we are part of the problem, and therefore we may also be in trouble!"

The guards picked up the cages and tossed them onto wheeled carts. The lab technician punched a code into the keypad next to the door. The lab doors glided open. The guards rolled the carts into the hallway toward the elevator. One of the guards pressed the "up" elevator call button. There was a loud *ding* and the button light went off. The doors slid open as elevator music spilled into the hallway. They maneuvered the carts onto the elevator. They had some difficulty rolling the wheels over the uneven threshold. The carts jerked and finally jumped into place. The doors closed with a quiet *whoosh* and a soft *thud.* One of the guards pressed the button for the 3rd floor. He complained how the elevator sucked, because the floor threshold was never even when you tried to roll a cart on or off them.

"Pepper, we're going up. We've never been there before. I don't like this!"

The elevator bounced to a stop. The doors opened and the guards rolled the dogs down the hallway into a large conference room.

Dr. Seymour Gore directed the guards to place the carts by the row of windows. The dogs peered out at the front side of the "Aging Research Institute" (ARI) building. In reality, ARI was a secret government research lab, disguised as an institute engaged in aging research. It was situated on a wooded hilltop, and overlooked a massive shopping mall and Highway 101. Marshy wetlands and San Pablo Bay were visible beyond the highway. A large, black SUV rolled to a halt at the ARI entrance. The "NIA" seal was stenciled on the front doors.

"Look, Pepper. It says "NIA" on that car's door."

"Uh, oh Buddy. They're the people Dr. Gore feared were coming here. And since we are at this meeting, it looks like we're right in the middle of the trouble too!"

Three people walked toward the front entrance of the ARI building. Their heads were down and they strode with a quick and purposeful gait.

Minutes later, the three unsmiling people came through the third-floor conference room doorway. Dr. Gore rushed over and extended his hand to greet the guests. All three of the NIA executives ignored his extended hand and chose seats together at the huge conference table.

"Buddy, this meeting looks like it is going to be worse than Dr. Gore imagined."

Dr. Gore smiled as he welcomed his guests and said, "Please help yourselves to coffee, tea, water and cookies." He pointed to the table against the rear wall.

The burly gray-haired man from NIA looked up with a scowl. He waved his hand dismissively. "Dr. Gore, forget the friendly chit chat and let's get on with the meeting."

Dr. Gore winced from the rebuke, cleared his throat and said, "Yes, yes, of course, sir."

He pressed a button on the remote control that closed the window blinds and lowered the projector screen.

"Pepper, he's not a nice man. His name should be Mr. Gnarly."

Pepper laughed and then listened closely to the discussion.

Dr. Gore's right eyebrow twitched several times as he told his guests, "We have our two most advanced dogs here, should you want a demonstration of their capabilities. We are certain you will be impressed with how well these dogs perform, and with the progress of the overall research project."

Mr. Gnarly snorted, "Now that would be a pleasant surprise! However, I don't think we want to waste time with any more of your dog tricks right now!"

Mr. Gnarly's two colleagues looked down at their papers on the table. They covered their laughter with coughs and hid growing smirks with their hands.

Dr. Gore's hand convulsed as he clicked past the "Welcome NIA" slide. He paused on a slide titled "Project Spy-Dogs."

"Gentlemen, if you would allow me to give a brief review of the project."

"Make it quick, Gore!"

The image showed Dr. Gore in an operating room implanting special brain wave sensors, advanced computer and cellular chips into Buddy and Pepper. Other slides showed lab scientists uploading software into the computers that were concealed in the dogs' heads. The next slide triggered a video that showed Buddy and Pepper in their special lab cages learning English and Spanish words and watching videos to learn about the outside environment.

Buddy and Pepper watched and listened as Dr. Gore explained how he had created these genetically engineered, computer-enhanced dogs. Dr. Gore felt more relaxed and confident when talking about the details of his research project. He beamed with pride and boasted, "I designed the computer chips, the software and the language training programs that has made all of this possible."

"Yes, yes. We are all aware of your brilliant accomplishments, Dr. Gore," Mr. Gnarly said sarcastically.

Dr. Gore winced hearing Mr. Gnarly's thinly veiled insult. He forced a smile and said, "I call these dogs my iMutts , because of all the advanced computers, cellular communications processors and the software in their bodies."

Dr. Gore paused, but none of the NIA guests smiled, much less laughed at his quip. Gore cleared his throat, and advanced to the next slide. His hands had become moist and shaky and he almost dropped the remote control.

"The most important breakthrough was linking their brainwave patterns to the computer's English/Spanish dictionary so we can convert their thoughts to text. This has taken hundreds of training sessions to accomplish, but is now quite reliable. Soon NIA will be able to use my iMutts as effective and reliable spy dogs. My iMutts can send text messages, e-mails and videos to NIA agents, to report their first hand surveillance observations."

"Pepper, did you hear that? Dr. Gore has been training us to be spies. And did you see all the stuff he surgically implanted into our bodies, to read our thoughts and enable us to send text messages? Pepper, we're freaks of some sort. We're Frankensteins or maybe Frankendogs!"

Pepper was silent. She wondered what would happen next.

Mr. Gnarly interrupted Dr. Gore. "Look Gore, we have been through all this before. You claim these iMutts of yours will be ready soon, but 'soon' never seems to arrive."

"We need a little more time to make them field ready."

"We're tired of all your lame promises and excuses. Frankly, we are more excited about some of the new spy drones we have developed. Did you know we now have a drone the size of a hummingbird, that can capture and transmit audio and video images back to our NIA agents from almost anywhere? We're no longer convinced your spy-dog project will be as useful to us. The drones are cheaper, just as effective and they're available for use NOW!"

"But your drones can't think! The iMutts are more effective than those flying robots. The dogs can get very close to the people you want to watch. And they understand what information is important. No, your drones are just flying bugs; machines that can't think."

"Well that remains to be seen Gore. I'm sorry, but unless you can deploy these iMutts of yours for a full field trial within three months, we'll have to shut down your project."

Dr. Gore's face turned red. He sputtered, "That's not p ... p ... possible yet! But, but, but wait!"

"Sorry Gore, no buts about it. We came here to work out a plan to complete your research during the next three months and get your iMutts into service. However, now if you say it's not possible in that amount of time, we'll have to shut down your research project sooner! Money doesn't grow on trees, you know. I think one month should give you adequate time to reassign your research staff and dispose of the animals!"

"Wait, let's not be hasty. I'll find a way. You have to give me a chance!"

"I don't have to do anything Gore. But okay, I'll give you three months. We'll meet again in thirty days, and I better see major progress or else!"

On a signal from Mr. Gnarly, the meeting ended. All of the NIA people stood up and left the conference room. They hurried to the waiting limousine that would take them to the airport for their return flight to Washington, DC on a plush NIA jet.

After the NIA executives departed, a very agitated Dr. Gore met with his top researchers in the conference room.

"You heard what those idiots said! We'll have to speed up the program by at least six months!"

"But Dr. Gore, we're making as much progress as we can. We've even started training the dogs on two shifts. I don't think we can push them any harder."

"I'll do the thinking here, Whitman. There's always a way."

"Pepper, it sounds like Dr. Gore is panicked!"

Gore turned his back on his colleagues and stared out of the window at the bay. He put the palm of his hand onto his now sweaty forehead and then smoothed his thinning hair as he pondered. He pivoted back toward his staff with his index finger pointed upward as he said, "I have it!"

"What is it, Dr. Gore?"

"We'll operate on the dogs and implant the new, more powerful experimental computer chips."

"But Dr. Gore, those chips have not been fully tested and the operation will be too dangerous. There's a fifty percent chance the animals will die from the operation!"

"Well that's a chance we'll have to take! We'll schedule the operation for three days from today."

"Pepper, what does he mean 'WE' have to take the chance? He's not the one who may die from the operation."

The researcher made a final plea, "Shouldn't we discuss this a little more before we decide to move forward?"

"No! No more discussion is necessary. Now return the iMutts to the lab and prepare the new devices."

"Pepper, I think we are in big trouble!"

"It doesn't look good, Buddy. Maybe we should see what Sean Keegan thinks."

Pepper texted Sean, whose e-mail and cell phone contact information she and Buddy had captured weeks before:

Sean, the NIA people say they will shut down Dr. Gore's research program and 'dispose of' us, unless we are 'field ready' in three months. They gave him one month to show 'major' progress. Dr. Gore is going to implant us with new experimental computer chips. His staff says the operation is too risky. Gore scheduled it to happen in three days. Are we in trouble? What should we do?

Pepper received a reply minutes later as the guards returned the dogs to the lab.

"Pepper, this situation is out of control. You and Buddy are in danger. We have to get you out of this lab as soon as possible. I'm working on an escape plan. See you both later. Sean."

4. Social justice

One week had passed since Alex's near drowning. He was still angry about what Bart had done, but what could he do about it? Given Bart's size and his reputation as a bully, Alex was afraid to challenge him. This whole revenge business required a careful strategy. That afternoon Alex went to swimming practice. Most of his friends had forgotten what had happened or had moved onto some new topic or victim. Well, Alex had not moved on. He pondered how he could return the favor to Bart, as he changed into his swim trunks in the locker room. Alex headed toward the locker room exit, and Bart bumped into him hard.

"Out of my way Logan, you little derp!"

Bart elbowed past Alex in his usual brutish fashion and headed toward the bathroom in a big hurry. Alex noticed Bart had left his over-sized swim trunks on the bench near his locker. Someone had left the First-Aid kit opened on a nearby table. A roll of adhesive tape and a pair of scissors sat on the table next to the kit. An idea popped into Alex's mind from some dark and devious place. He picked up the scissors and raced over to Bart's locker. Alex looked around to be certain nobody else was nearby. He knew he didn't have much time and Bart could return at any moment. He pulled out the drawstring out of Bart's swim trunks and cut about 95% of the way through it. Alex carefully pulled the severed drawstring back into the swim trunks and placed them on the bench exactly as Bart had left them. Alex replaced the scissors and exited the locker room doorway to the pool, as Bart rushed back to his locker.

Alex headed straight to the diving board to have some fun, while everyone waited for Coach Fish to begin swimming practice. Bart rushed out of the locker room, tying his swim trunks. He looked up and saw Alex in line at the diving board. Bart ran to catch up with Alex and cut into the line right behind him.

Alex thought, Bart obviously intends to start swim practice today with a repeat performance of his killer cannonball at the last practice. Since coach Fish was busy talking to some other people, there would be nobody to stop him.

Alex thought, I'll be ready this time. As my dad often said, "Fool me once, shame on you; fool me twice, shame on me."

Alex walked out to the end of the diving board. The entire pool area became quieter. Alex noticed lots of people looked his way and seemed to be holding their breath. Bart was next in line and everyone anticipated what he planned to do. No stopping now, so Alex bounced on the diving board, sprang skyward. He did a perfect jackknife dive and entered the water with a tiny splash.

Alex thought; A perfect ten … No doubt about it! Alex looked up as he turned and moved toward the surface. He could see Bart looking down into the pool. Bart was calculating the perfect timing and spot to blast down on top of him. As Bart ran forward to launch himself from the diving board, Alex changed direction and swam downward and toward the pool wall under the diving board.

Bart bounced high and tucked his body into his dumb cannonball position. He soared outward toward the spot in the pool where Alex had previously been. *KABLOOM*, Bart hit the water hard, splashing water in every direction. Meanwhile, Alex swam, unscathed toward the ladder on the side of the pool. Bart surfaced looking around confused, because he had completely missed his target. He spotted Alex getting out of the pool and swam as fast as possible toward the pool ladder. Alex noticed

almost all eyes at the pool were locked onto the
unfolding drama.

Alex walked around to the diving board and
stood in line as Bart hurried up the ladder to get out
of the pool. Bart rushed up the ladder and pushed
himself upward out of the water with an angry and
powerful thrust. He rose with such force that the
drawstring on his over-sized swim trunks snapped
where Alex had cut it. Bart's swim trunks slipped
down to his knees. All of the kids in the pool area
gasped, and burst into the loudest waves of laughter
Alex had ever heard. Echoes of laughter bounced
around the enclosed pool area and amplified the
volume. Bart tried to pull up his wet and sagging
trunks, but he lost his balance on the ladder and fell
backwards into the pool. Bart swallowed some water
while he floundered and struggled to pull up his
trunks. He coughed and spit, much like Alex had the
previous week. He maneuvered with one arm back to
the ladder. Bart wobbled on the ladder step and lost
his balance again. He let go of his swim trunks and
grabbed for the ladder to avoid another fall into the
water. As he did so, his trunks once again fell down
to his knees. The girls swim team had entered the
pool area for their practice. There were high-pitched
screams mixed with even greater waves of laughter.

Bart pulled his trunks up, climbed out of the pool and rushed toward the boys' locker room. He was dripping wet and red-faced. He stumbled with an awkward gait as he held up his swim-trunks with one hand. The echoing sounds of laughter pursued him through the locker room door. Bart did not re-emerge from the locker room that afternoon.

Alex thought … Not only did Bart get what he deserved, he would never suspect I had anything to do with it. How sweet were revenge and justice?

Bart did not show up for the next swimming class. Alex's friend Jo said Bart had dropped out of swimming for the semester. Alex guessed that Bart was too embarrassed to show his face at the pool after his falling swim-trunks act.

Alex thought … Well it looks like swimming class is going to be OK after all.

Robert Healy

5. The great escape

Sean Keegan took his responsibilities as caretaker of the lab animals very seriously. He fed the animals, cleaned their cages and walked the dogs outside whenever he could sneak them out. However, Sean was actually an undercover spy for "People Interested in the Treatment of Animals" or PITA for short. PITA insisted that animals be bred and raised humanely. Their slogan was "Be PITA Bred." They assigned Sean to investigate possible animal abuse at the ARI laboratory.

After his text to Pepper, Sean put a plan to rescue the iMutts into motion. Sean pretended illness and went home mid-afternoon. He returned to ARI early that evening. Only a few people worked at the lab on Friday nights, so Sean would have easy access to the iMutts, once he got past the security guard at the front desk. Sean walked back into the Aging Research Institute lobby at 7:30 PM.

The security guard at the front desk said, "I can't let you into the labs after hours, Sean. I'm sorry, but I don't want to get into trouble."

Sean had anticipated the guard's response and said, "Okay, I understand your point, but, when Dr. Gore finds out his animals were not fed and their cages were not cleaned, he will be angry. And if the researchers can't complete their tasks with the dogs tomorrow, because you wouldn't let me into the lab tonight, you'll be the one in big trouble, dude. And you know how nasty Dr. Gore has been lately about any delays to his research schedule!"

The guard swallowed hard and shuffled some papers. He did not know what to say or do in this situation. Either way he would be in trouble. A few beads of perspiration ran down his forehead from his silly looking guard hat and nestled in his eyebrow. He struggled to regain the appearance of control and authority.

"Alright Keegan, just this one time, but you better be quick about it!"

"Don't worry. I'll be in and out in no time."

Sean took the elevator to the main lab facility on the second floor. He used his card key to open the research lab door and entered the room. He unlocked the iMutts' cages as fast as he could. Buddy and Pepper leaped out and greeted him with slurpy kisses. Sean lifted Buddy and Pepper onto a lab bench and connected one of the lab computers to the tiny USB fitting behind each dogs' ear. Sean scrolled through the "settings" menu, which was strikingly similar to standard iPhone and iPad menus. He turned off the GPS option to broadcast the dogs' location, so Dr. Gore would not be able to track them. Next he changed their computer password to "sean4dogs" to prevent Gore's people from remotely resetting their GPS broadcast settings. He told the dogs the new password in case they needed to make other computer modifications later.

The sleepy ARI security guard on the first floor watched a basketball game on TV, instead of looking at the video images on the bank of security monitors. His favorite team scored a three point shot to take the lead with only seconds left in the game. The guard pumped his fist in the air and hollered, "Yes!" He glanced over at the security monitors and spotted Sean with the dogs out of their cages in the second floor research lab. He hit the alarm button to alert the other security guards.

Sean heard the alarm. He burst through the lab door and ran to the emergency exit stairwell. He dashed down two steps at a time. Sean rushed through the stairwell door onto the first floor landing, with the iMutts tailing behind him. Two guards barged onto the landing from the lobby door. Sean pushed open the outside emergency exit door with a mighty heave. An alarm bell clanged loudly as the iMutts rushed through and escaped into the night.

6. iMutts on the run

The iMutts bolted through the emergency exit door and ran for their lives. They expected Sean Keegan to be right behind them. But the lab technician did not burst through the exit door to freedom. A burly guard had tackled him to the ground and restrained him. Sean had rescued Buddy and his sister Pepper from a likely death at the hands of Dr. Seymour Gore. The mad scientist had performed illegal surgeries and conducted unethical experiments in an attempt to turn the iMutts into spy dogs. But now, poor Sean would suffer grave consequences for his brave act. Dr. Gore's vengeance would be harsh.

Guards poured through the exit doorway in pursuit of the escaped dogs. They waved their flashlights across the research laboratory lawn. One of the guards spotted the red glow of Buddy and Pepper's eyes in the dark.

"There they are! Grab them!"

The security crew sprinted across the grass toward the dogs.

"Pepper, where's Sean?"

"Don't know. Can't help Sean now. We have to get out of here!"

"Right, but where to?"

"To the woods. We'll lose them!"

"Then what?" Buddy worried.

"We'll worry about that later."

The dogs sprinted into a protective patch of oak and bay trees, then bounded downhill weaving through heavy brush. The thick brush and rocks slowed the pace of the stumbling guards, who quickly gasped for breath. Their footfalls landed with clumsy thuds. Within minutes, the piercing beams of their flashlights receded from the fleeing dogs. Their pursuit had slowed to a crawl.

"Pepper, those fat guards are pathetic. They ate too many doughnuts, and watched too many hours of TV sitting on comfortable couches."

"Don't gloat so soon Buddy, we're not safe yet!"

The *whoosh* of fast moving traffic and the roar of truck engines filtered up from the highway below, and replaced the shouts of the winded guards.

The dogs worked their way downhill until they reached the shoulder of the freeway. At the bottom of the long hill, Buddy and Pepper faced a new threat, Highway 101. The busy six-lane freeway was the main artery through Marin County, in California.

"There's a huge shopping mall over there, Pepper, teeming with people and cars."

"We better avoid them. Let's go left."

They trotted north, away from the shopping plaza and the research lab.

"Where are all these cars and trucks going? Why is everyone going so fast?"

"I don't know Buddy, but they look like they're running away from somebody, just like we are!"

Blasts of wind buffeted the dogs, as the noisy traffic rumbled and whooshed past.

"Buddy, perhaps we should run to the other side to the open-space area. Maybe we will find a safe place to hide there."

"Let's go for it now! There's a break in traffic!"

The dogs took a few leaps out onto the highway. Bright lights quickly bore down on them with unexpected speed. Horns blasted angry warnings, as cars and trucks swerved to miss them. The dogs retreated to the shoulder.

"Those cars almost killed us Buddy," Pepper said, trembling.

Buddy's fur stood on end. "I'm not sure which is more dangerous, Dr. Gore and his goons or the stampeding traffic on Highway 101!"

"We need to find another way across. This is way too dangerous."

"We're lucky to be alive, Pepper. Wherever we go today, I feel like somebody or something is trying to kill us."

"We can't stay here and be spotted. Those guards may not be far behind! We have to do something!"

"Let's walk along the tree line, where we can't be seen. Maybe we'll find a safer way, like an overpass."

As they trotted further north, Pepper said, "What's that noise?"

Two police cars roared by with their sirens screaming and their lights flashing. The dogs scrambled further into the woods and hid.

"Stop shaking Pepper, you're making me nervous."

"Those police cars may be looking for us!"

"How do you know?"

"I don't, but we can't take any chances. We have to find a good place to hide, and soon!"

A few exits north, they came to a storm pipe that passed under the road. They were now several miles north of the secret research lab.

"Pepper, I bet this storm pipe goes to the other side of the highway."

"Let's give it a try."

They trotted down the embankment to the entrance of the cement storm-pipe. Only a trickle of water currently drained through the four-foot diameter pipe. They walked in and went under the highway. Traffic rumbled overhead. The entire pipe vibrated from the speed and weight of the cars and trucks passing over it.

"Pepper, let's move faster, this pipe feels like it's going to collapse!"

The pipe ended at a pond. They looked across thirty yards of water at the dry ground beyond the pond, and shook their heads.

"Uh oh, Buddy, a dead end. Look at all that water. We've never learned how to swim! Maybe we should turn around."

"Come on Pepper, this is no biggie. We've watched plenty of videos of animals swimming. It can't be that hard. We can do this."

"I hope you're right!"

They waded into the water and paddled their legs, like they were running.

"See Pepper, we're moving toward dry land."

"So far, so good."

The water became shallower and their feet touched the bottom. They walked out of the water for the last ten feet and onto the pond bank. They were soaked, cold, lost pups, but they were encouraged by their cleverness and bravery. They shook their bodies and a spray of water flew outward from their furry coats.

"Hey Pepper, that was fun. Let's do it again." Buddy stepped toward the pond.

"We don't have time for fun now! We have to find a safe place to sleep."

Pepper led them toward the open-space, and further away from the secret government lab.

They ran for another thirty minutes, until they felt safe. No one had pursued them. They found a quiet place among a grove of oak trees and stopped to rest. They were frightened, from all that had happened to them. Could they survive in the wild and avoid capture? Why had their comfortable lives been turned upside down? Would they ever enjoy a peaceful life again, now that they were runaway fugitives? Neither dog had good answers, only more questions. They shivered with cold and fright.

7. Zygor versus math homework

Sunday afternoon, Alex's mom told him to go to his room and finish his homework assignments before he would be allowed to watch any more TV.

Alex protested, "I already know all that stuff and it's boring."

"If you already know 'All that stuff,' it won't take you long to do. So, get up there and finish your homework. Then, you can do whatever you want."

"OK, OK, I'm on it," Alex said, unconvincingly.

Alex moped up the stairs to his room. He slumped over to his bed, grabbed his backpack and removed a schoolbook and a lined pad. He shuffled to his desk, slapped the books onto the desktop and dropped hard onto his chair with exasperation. He groaned his with frustration. Alex flipped open his math book and it nudged his computer mouse. The computer display blinked on. A graphic of the moon, Mortu appeared, where Alex had paused his game of "Dark Star Warrior – The Rebellion." Mortu stared back at him, begging him to come back and play. Alex looked at his opened math book and then back at the game screen. He remembered he had paused the game near the final level and possible victory over Zygor the Terrible.

Alex closed his schoolbook, shoved it aside and clicked the mouse to resume the saved game. He paused to remember what was going on during his last game session. Alex had landed on Mortu, the largest of the three moons orbiting the planet Gorn. He resumed his quest.

His feet crunched on the lifeless surface of Mortu. Careful, because each step might be his last. He was totally focused on his survival in this strange and foreboding place. Hot, smelly looking gases spurted up from cracks in the barren soil under his feet. No birds appeared in Mortu's vacant, yellow sky. Not even a lizard scurried across the scorched rocks beneath his feet. Alex heard the constant hiss of hot gases escaping from the parched, cracked surface of Mortu. Once in a while, a trans-orbital freighter passed overhead on its way to Nebulon. It carried a valuable load of Mortu's Kraznium ore, the finest in the galaxy. Kraznium had become the greatest energy source in the galaxy and was the source of the wealth and power of Zygor, the evil emperor of the Gorn people.

Alex had already defeated Glubar, a powerful Gorn warlord and the strongest ally of Zygor. Glubar had lured Alex to this desolate moon and had set a clever trap that Alex had almost fallen for. Alex saw an atomic Taser sitting on the ground next to a large boulder. His game avatar stepped forward to examine it. He reached down for the Taser, but at the last instant, Alex noticed a flash of light to his left. It was a reflection from Glubar's face-shield. Alex dove for cover behind a nearby boulder as Glubar's anti-matter phaser vaporized the ground where Alex had just stood. The blast turned the ground into a gaping, steaming, five-foot hole. Glubar would fire another shot as soon as his phaser weapon recharged. Alex shouldered his proton thruster and aimed it in the direction of Glubar's last shot. In nanoseconds, the computer in Alex's weapon calculated Glubar's location and fired a lethal proton beam. An intense pink streak of supercharged protons flashed toward Glubar. He ducked too late, and was vaporized into a pale, rosy cloud of sub-atomic particles that drifted upward toward the cosmic void.

A game message appeared. It told Alex he had earned 100,000 Zirconian Parsecs for his victory.

A bead of sweat trickled down Alex's neck. His hand relaxed on the game controller and he shook his head, gasped, and re-gripped the device. He wiped his brow and refocused on the game mission. He scanned the landscape for other threats and saw none. He looked at the map in the front pocket of his Galactic Good Guys uniform. He still had to navigate through the dangerous Trans-Mordial swamp, beyond the mountain range on the west side of this desert. He needed to reach the Inter-Galactic wormhole on the other side of the swamp. The wormhole was a portal to a future dimension. There he could obtain the advanced weapons he needed to defeat Zygor and free the enslaved people of Gorn. Alex had never gotten this far! Maybe nobody had. None of his friends had ever defeated Zygor. One false step or one lapse in his attention could result in his quick but painless death. Alex's defeat would doom the people of Gorn to suffering under the tyranny of Zygor, perhaps forever.

Alex crossed the mountains at the western end of the desert and on the other side, the swamp stretched out below him. It dared him to approach. Green vapors rose into the thin moon air, as swamp ooze bubbles reached the surface and *plopped* when they burst. Alex worked his way down the steep, rocky slope to the swamp. He looked at his map again to determine the exact location of the wormhole. He checked his weapons and took a bold but frightened step forward. He was up to his knees in steamy, murky swamp ooze. Alex focused on the surface in front of him. He watched for hungry crocks and huge Anaconda snakes. Alex heard a low, sub-human growl, and noticed motion to his right. A Cosmotic Swamp Creature leaped toward him out of the green Trans-Mordial ooze. Alex's mom put her hand on his shoulder as he turned and aimed his Ion Blaster to vaporize the swamp creature. Alex flinched. His shot missed, high right. The swamp creature bellowed a laugh. Alex heard a vicious, inhuman roar as the massive swamp creature devoured his game avatar in one bite. A message popped up on Alex's computer screen:

"You are now dead Alex Logan. Zygor fears no mortal. Better luck next time. Zygor waits for you."

Alex screamed, "Mom! Look what you have done! I almost completed level six, so I could move to level seven where I could have defeated Zygor, the Evil Emperor of Gorn. Nobody has ever done that! You ruined everything!"

"Well, Alex, I guess the people of Gorn will have to wait one more day to be freed from Zygor the

Terrible, because you are supposed to finish your homework! Now, shut down that game and fire up your homework."

"Why do I have to do this stupid homework now? Why can't I do it later!"

"Because now is much better, and NOW is when you said you would do it. No further negotiations, Mister. Get busy!"

Alex reluctantly dragged out his math textbook and his homework assignment. He turned the pages to find the right chapter. Alex thought how lame these math word problems were. He made up a 'mock' word problem, as he flipped through the math textbook:

Interstate highway 80 stretches 2,900 miles from San Francisco to Teaneck, NJ.

A car leaves downtown San Francisco on Route 80 traveling east at 65 miles per hour. At the same time, another car leaves Teaneck, NJ on Route 80 traveling west at 75 miles per hour.

How long will it take for both drivers to get a speeding ticket?

For extra credit, which driver gets their speeding ticket first?

Alex enjoyed a quiet laugh at his clever "mock" word problem. Then he read his first real math homework problem with much less enthusiasm. He sharpened his pencil, wrote the number one in the margin of the homework paper. He circled the number to procrastinate further. His Mom hovered nearby. Alex dreamed of defeating Zygor.

Robert Healy

8. Safe, but for how long?

Buddy and Pepper were lucky that Sean had responded so quickly save them from Dr. Seymour Gore and his henchmen. They hoped Sean was safe, but they worried because it appeared he had not escaped from the guards. They were in no position to help their friend Sean, because they still needed to find a safe place where the NIA agents and ARI could not find them. They also needed to figure out how to survive in the wild.

Buddy and Pepper had traveled several miles away from the ARI building. They felt safe, for the moment, but soon Dr. Gore and the NIA would send people to recapture them. It would be easier for the NIA agents to spot them in the daylight, so they had to find a better place to hide, far away from their pursuers.

"Pepper, what are we going to do now? We can't stay here for long, because we're not far enough away from ARI yet."

"I'm not sure Buddy. We've never been off the ARI lab property before much less having to live on our own in the woods."

"Let's ask Sean Keegan, Pepper; he may know what to do!"

"Okay, I'll text him now."

Pepper received a reply a few minutes after she sent a text to Sean:

"Sean is in custody. We are coming to get you. You cannot escape. We will find you wherever you run. Make it easy on yourselves. Give up now and all will be forgiven."

"Pepper, do you think they mean it? I mean the forgiveness part. It's scary out here and we don't know how to hunt."

"Are you kidding? They are treacherous liars. We can't trust people! Especially those people!"

"But, what about Sean? He helped us!"

"Sean may be the exception. Nevertheless, the rule is, don't trust people! We have to make it on our own now, Buddy."

The iMutts resumed their frantic flight. They crossed back to the western side of the highway through another storm drain. They felt safer in the thicker, deep woods to the west of Olympali State Park. They ran deep into the forest. They were uncertain about exactly where to go, but their goal was to get far away as possible from the dreaded ARI lab and Dr. Gore. After two more hours of running through hills, woods and underbrush, the dogs paused, exhausted.

"Buddy, the ARI security guards will probably give up their search until morning, because of darkness. We should sleep now, so we are rested and can get further away tomorrow before the early-morning light."

"Great idea. I'm exhausted!"

Buddy and Pepper curled up next to each other under an oak tree and fell fast asleep. But they both slept uneasily. The iMutts twitched and made soft crying sounds. They both dreamt about their narrow escape from the lab … of the angry guards thrashing through the underbrush close behind them … of almost being run over crossing Highway 101.

They awakened with a start and jerked their heads up in alarm. Their eyes snapped wide open and their ears stood up when they heard scuffling noises nearby. A twig snapped. A chorus of yelping sounds began as the shuffling sounds increased in volume and frequency. The sounds seemed to come from all around them in the dense early morning fog. A shape emerged from the fog, then another and another. Coyotes! The pack of hungry coyotes whooped and barked in an eerie chorus. Their exposed fangs dripped with saliva. Three, four now five of the scrawny creatures had surrounded them. They moved in slow lurching strides, their heads low, as they encircled the iMutts. The coyote leader stopped. He sneered at the dogs and spoke in a voice dripping with sarcasm.

"Well, well, well, what have we here? A couple of tasty house pets, I'd say. What a treat, so well fed and tender. You shouldn't have come out here, where real animals live! There are no bags of kibble here. You have to eat what you can catch!"

"We don't mean you any harm," Buddy lamely suggested.

"Oh my, that's a relief," the coyote leader said. "We were so frightened; right guys?"

The other coyotes laughed.

The coyote leader continued his sarcasm, "We came over here to invite you newcomers to dinner; and guess what? You're it!"

The rest of the pack laughed hysterically, which pleased the leader.

Buddy and Pepper were larger than the wild coyotes, but they could not match them in speed, strength or numbers. They could not chase away five hungry critters and there was nowhere to run. Buddy and Pepper instinctively positioned themselves head to tail so at least one of them could defend against an attack from any direction. This seemed to excite the coyotes further. They sensed a quick fight, an imminent victory and a fine meal. They tightened their circle. The coyote leader turned and charged, but then he stopped and pulled back. He had faked the charge to see how the dogs would react, measuring how best to strike a fatal blow. The rest of the pack whooped and yelped at a frantic level. Buddy and Pepper sensed an attack would come at any moment.

The coyotes stopped circling. They jerked their heads up and turned toward the fog-shrouded underbrush. A pack of six large dogs crashed through the brush, and headed straight toward the out-numbered coyotes. The coyote leader understood the changed situation. He wasted no time and raced away from the oncoming dogs. The rest of the coyote pack ceased their yelping and followed the leader with their tails tucked between their legs. The dog pack raced past the iMutts in hot pursuit of the coyotes. Buddy and Pepper stood frozen in place, amazed at their good luck. The dogs chased the coyotes a short distance to be certain the critters would be too frightened to return and challenge the dogs.

The dog pack leader stopped, barked a few fierce final warnings, which meant, "And you better not come back here."

Satisfied that the coyotes were no longer a threat; the pack leader trotted over to Buddy and Pepper. The rest of the pack followed and looked at the pitiful, shaking newcomers.

The pack leader spoke first. "What in the world are you doing out here? And only two of you! Those miserable creatures would have eaten you!"

Buddy puffed his chest out and said, "We're glad you came along, but we could have handled those coyotes."

Pepper interrupted, "No we couldn't have. You saved our lives. Thank you."

"At least one of you has some sense and shows a little gratitude. I'm Molly. So what are you doing out here?"

"It's sort of a long story," said Pepper.

"Well, make it short then."

Pepper and Buddy blurted out their story of imprisonment and near-death in Dr. Gore's secret lab and how they escaped with the help of Sean Keegan and had been on the run ever since.

Molly listened carefully, and said, "Looks like you two need someone to save your lives quite regularly. I don't think you want to be on your own out here. We are only able to survive because we are a pack. Together we hunt and protect each other. Alone, we would not stand a chance. You can join up with us, if you want to?"

Pepper and Buddy looked at each other and blurted out, "Yes, can we? Thank you."

For the moment, the iMutts' situation looked much better.

Molly turned, and said, "Alright then, follow us."

Buddy and Pepper happily trotted off with their newfound family.

9. The roundup

For the next two days, Buddy and Pepper became friends with Molly and the other five members of the pack. All the pack dogs were older than Buddy and Pepper, who were only two years old. Several of the larger pack dogs weighed 75 to 100 pounds each. Marcel was a small "lap dog". They called him "The Runt". Buddy and Pepper each weighed 65 pounds, and were almost fully-grown. The pack showed the iMutts where the ponds, streams and water holes were located, and how to smell their way to find water when necessary. They learned how to hunt small critters with the pack. The pack used their numbers to flush out some poor creature, surround it and make the catch. But the dogs were neither as quick nor as good at hunting as the cunning coyotes. So, whenever possible, they would steal a meal from a lone coyote or two, when the pack of dogs could chase them away from their catch. They learned to stay away from camping and picnic areas in the daytime, because campers and hikers became alarmed at the sight of a pack of "wild dogs". People almost always reported dogs to the

Park Rangers. Sometimes teams of rangers would be sent to capture them using nets and tranquilizer darts.

On the third day, they hunted for rabbits in a low brushy area, near the Bay. They heard a rhythmic "*thwop, thwop, thwop*" beat. The sound seemed to come from all around them. Buddy looked up and saw three helicopters approaching from the Bay side. The aircraft hung in the morning sky and grew larger as they raced toward the dogs.

Molly recognized danger and warned all of the dogs to run for the woods as fast as possible. The helicopters descended upon them in minutes. They landed with a soft thud on the moist bay soil. The helicopters landed in a pattern that surrounded the dogs, and trapped them inside. The men hunted in packs and encircled their prey, just like coyotes and dogs. Men dressed in tan uniforms with an NIA patch on their shoulders burst from the aircrafts' side doors. Some of the men had rifles and others had large nets. One man pointed his rifle at a black dog that looked a bit like Buddy and Pepper. He pulled the trigger and the gun popped. A dart streaked out and lodged in the dog's hip. The dog ran a few steps and then sagged and fell motionless to the wet ground. A man ran over and secured the dog with plastic ties, which he placed on the dog's legs and snout. The man with the rifle found another victim nearby. He raised his rifle, sighted Pepper and took a step forward. He snagged his foot on a root, tripped and fell down. His gun discharged, but the dart landed harmlessly in the ground in front of him. He got up, but cursed because the dog had run beyond the range of his dart-gun. The dogs scattered, and raced in a variety of directions to confuse their would-be captors. The men managed to capture only one dog. They were unable to move quickly enough in the soft, muddy soil, so all of the other dogs escaped unharmed. The men vowed things would be different, the next time!

The dogs ran to the safety of the thick woods, where they reunited under the cover of the forest canopy. Molly had seen the men capture Max in the wetland area. They threw him into one of their helicopters. She was thankful the rest of the pack had escaped unharmed.

One of the pack, a dog named Tucker, said, "That was too close! Who were those people?"

Pepper responded, "I'm afraid they were after me and Buddy."

"How do you know that?" asked Molly.

"She's right," said Buddy. "They were people from the secret government lab we had escaped from. They said they would be coming after us!"

Tucker and another dog complained that Buddy and Pepper had put the whole pack in danger.

One dog yelled, "Look what happened to Max! We're not safe anymore with these two here."

"Yeah, they have to leave the pack," said another.

Pepper and Buddy dropped their heads and tails in shame.

Then Molly spoke in a firm and steady voice, "Look! We are never safe. There is always danger from coyotes and mountain lions. And people have tried to catch us long before Pepper and Buddy joined us. Two fewer dogs in the pack won't make us safer. And besides, those people will come back anyway to look for Buddy and Pepper. They won't know our two new friends are no longer with us. We have to be extra careful for a while, until they give up their search, and they will. We'll go up into the hills on the West side of the highway where there are more trees and places to hide. Meanwhile, we can't expel Buddy and Pepper from the pack, because it would be a death sentence for them. We have to be brave and stick together. We are a family and we must protect each other."

The other dogs hung their heads and muttered that Molly was right. Buddy and Pepper apologized for bringing trouble to the pack, and swore they would do anything to help Max return to the pack.

The dogs crossed an underpass beneath highway 101. They trotted away from the helicopters, toward the hills and the deep forest on the other side.

"Thank you Molly," Buddy said. "That was kind and brave of you to help us, when the other dogs were so frightened."

"We must keep the pack together. It is the only way we can survive. Make sure you two work extra hard and make a contribution to our pack."

Molly trotted ahead.

Buddy shook his head. "Wow she is some leader, isn't she?"

Pepper's gaze followed Molly. "Yes she is, but did you notice the USB connector wire protruding from behind her ear? It was just like ours?"

Robert Healy

10. The sports book

Alex was in his room finishing his homework. He had learned his lesson about playing video games before doing his homework assignments. He opened his math workbook, and thought; More stupid math problems, what a bore. You have to be a total dweeb to like this stuff.

His phone blurted out his favorite ringtone. Alex looked at the phone and saw it was his friend Zoo calling. He put the call on speaker.

"Yo-yo Zoo-man! How's life?"

"No worries man. What's happening?"

"Nothin. What's up with you?"

Alex's sister Savannah wandered into Alex's room while he was talking.

"Nothin. Hey, I'm just calling in my bet for tomorrow's games, man."

"Sure Zoo, what players do you want?"

"I'm taking Cabrera, Trout and Molina tomorrow for $2.00 … and you are going down, man."

"We'll see." Alex repeated the bet and said, "You're on … and good luck, dude."

Back to the dreaded math homework … Alex's phone rang again. This time it was his friend Jo.

"Hey Jo, what's going on?"

"Nothin. Hey, I have a bet for Thursday. OK?"

"No problema, Jo. Who do you want?"

"How about Mauer, Johnson and Wirth for $3.00?"

"Hey, that's your call, dude." Alex repeated the bet and said, "Great, your bet is on … and good luck man. Ciao."

Savannah shook her head. "Hey Alex, what's with the bets?"

"What do you want, Savannah?"

"OH, I just came in to ask to borrow some paper. But this betting thing, what's up with that?"

"If you must know, Miss Snoopy, I invented this way cool baseball betting game. People bet me that the three Major League baseball players they pick will get a total of five or more hits among them on a given day. If they do it, they win the bet. If not, I win. I did the research and the math and figured out that I should win two out of three times."

"But Alex, aren't you taking advantage of your friends?"

"Hey, they have a chance to win and they don't have to make the bets. It's cool and so far I'm way ahead."

"Does Mom know you're doing this?"

"Nah. And you better not tell her. This is between me and the guys."

"I won't tell, but I think you're taking a big chance. This might get you into trouble."

"Chill, Savannah. Everything is under control. You worry too much."

Alex returned to his homework, but couldn't wait be done with it, so he could fire up the game console and Mine Craft.

11. Max returns

The day after Max was abducted, the dogs gathered together deep inside of a redwood forest. They finished off the last bits of two unfortunate rabbits. Two dogs stretched out and yawned. Another dog scratched her back against a fallen log. Then all the dogs stood, pricked up their ears on full alert. They looked downhill toward the stream that meandered through the redwood grove. Surprised and delighted, they watched Max trot happily toward them with his tail wagging. The pack erupted in celebration of Max's miraculous return. The dogs barked loudly and raced around Max. Their tails wagged with joy, all except Molly. She stood in place and stared at Max's neck. Molly interrupted the celebration with a loud bark. The dogs focused on Molly.

Tucker said, "Hurray, Max is back! What?"

Molly asked, "Max, where did you get the new collar?"

"The men put it on me before they let me go. Pretty cool huh?"

Molly, Pepper and Buddy examined Max's collar.

Buddy noticed a blinking red light. "It's a tracking collar. They are using it to find out where we are hiding."

Pepper said, "We have to remove it now. It may already be too late."

Buddy chewed at the collar with rapid bites. He was more than halfway through the collar when the dogs heard the first drone of engines in the distance.

"They're coming," Molly shouted. "I can hear their machines. Get that collar off now!"

Buddy chewed as fast as he could. Finally, the collar fell to the ground. The screaming engine sounds were close now. Men riding on All Terrain Vehicles (ATV's) came into view.

Pepper told Molly, "Take the pack to safety, while Buddy and I lead the men away in the opposite direction."

Pepper picked up the collar in her mouth and ran up the hill deeper into the redwood grove with Buddy right behind her. Molly and the rest of the pack ran downhill toward a nearby oak forest and heavy brush. Buddy barked and one of the men spotted him. The ATV's turned uphill in pursuit of the iMutts. Buddy and Pepper emerged from the trees into a small clearing. They stopped for a moment to decide where to run next. As they did, two of the ATV's roared into the clearing from opposite sides and headed straight for the iMutts, who stood frozen in fear. One of the men raised a dart pistol. As he was about to pull the trigger, his ATV hit a concealed rock. The jolt caused his finger to pull the trigger before the gun was properly aimed. A tranquilizer dart flew wildly off-target and embedded into the shoulder of the man driving the other ATV. The shocked man slowed his machine, grabbed at the dart and pulled it out, but too late. He stood up and swung his leg off the ATV. He staggered as the tranquilizer drug took effect. The man stumbled. His body sagged and he fell to the ground with a thud, face down and unconscious. The shooter's ATV bounced out of control and struck a tree stump. The rider hurtled over the windshield into the woods and tumbled down a steep slope.

Buddy and Pepper ran further uphill on a rock-strewn slope. They hoped the other men would have trouble following on their ATV's. They ran to the scrubby brush area above the clearing as two more ATV's appeared and headed in their direction. The iMutts ran nimbly up the rocky slope. The men were forced to abandon their ATV's halfway up, because of the steepness of the hill and the rocks. They jumped off their machines two hundred feet below the dogs and continued their pursuit on foot. The iMutts raced up the slope but the sparse brush provided minimal cover. Pepper spotted a large rock outcropping near the top of the hill. A cave opening became visible as they drew nearer. The entrance was large enough for them to enter, but was probably too small for the men.

"Pepper, maybe we can hide in there."

"I'm not sure that's a good idea, Buddy, because we could become trapped."

"Let's check it out."

They ran to the cave opening, while the men struggled up the steep slope below them. The strong scent of some sort of animal came from the opening. The dogs crept into the cave, wary of possible danger. They heard a fierce growl followed by a shrieking sound as they rounded the first turn in the rock entrance. A mountain lioness and her young cub crouched at the rear of the small cave. The lioness bared her fangs, ready to protect her cub from the intruders. Pepper dropped the tracking collar she had held in her mouth during the chase. It settled into the soft dirt floor of the lion's den. The dogs apologized and backed out of the den entrance and fled before the lion attacked. They scrambled out of the cave and bolted unseen up the slope behind the rock outcropping. The dogs crested the hill and ran down the other side, into the cover of the forest below. The men were busy clawing up the slope and did not notice the dogs escape.

The iMutts cringed when they heard a loud motor sound that shook the air around them. The now familiar "*thwop, thwop, thwop*" beat of helicopter blades, shattered the quiet forest landscape. A sleek, black aircraft became visible as it hovered like a bird of prey over the rock outcropping and the lion's den. The two men chasing the iMutts on foot, reached the rock cave entrance. One of the men held a computer device with a map display. It tracked the signal broadcasted by Max's electronic dog collar. The pilot of the helicopter radioed to the men on the ground, confirming that the tracking collar signal came from the rocks in front of them.

One of the men said, "We have them now. It looks like they are hiding in this rock cave."

"Good, they're trapped," said the other fellow. "I guess these dogs are not so smart after all."

"OK, load your dart gun and let's go. It looks like it's going to be a bad day for two very bad dogs."

The men moved a few loose rocks away from the entrance, so the opening became large enough for one of the men to crawl into the cave. The smaller of the two men removed his dart gun from its holster, loaded it and crawled into the cave on his stomach, holding a small flashlight. He went a few feet into the passage and saw the red dog collar lying on the ground. He reached his hand forward and grasped the collar. He heard a low, powerful growl, and looked up into the fiery eyes and bared fangs of an angry mountain lion. The man screamed and frantically tried to back out of the cave entrance. He raised his dart gun and shot. The dart bounced harmlessly off the rock ceiling of the cave. His partner sensed something had gone wrong. He grabbed the back of his partner's NIA vest and pulled his friend out of the cave. The smaller man screamed and ran down the slope. When his partner saw the lion's head appear at the cave entrance, he too turned and ran in panic. Both men stumbled, tripped, fell, ripped their clothing and screamed for help at the top of their lungs.

Meanwhile Buddy and Pepper safely worked their way down to the valley below and followed a stream for several miles. They stopped for a drink of water and rested. The men from NIA were far behind them and no longer a threat, at least for now.

Buddy and Pepper walked through the woods until they picked up the scent of their pack. They followed the scent for an hour and then caught sight of their friends. Buddy barked and ran, tail wagging. Molly spotted Pepper and Buddy, and waited for them to rejoin the group.

Buddy told the pack about the men on ATV's, the chase, and how they tricked the men into the lion's den while they made their escape. Buddy described how the men ran for their lives down the slope away from the mountain lion. The dogs all laughed and said how brave Buddy was to have faced a lion and escaped from the evil men. Buddy enjoyed every moment of their attention. He felt heroic.

Meanwhile, Pepper and Molly slowly walked away from the other dogs to have a quiet chat.

"OK, what happens next, Molly?"

"How would I know?"

"Because, unless I am wrong, you have gone through this before. Right?"

"Why do you say that Pepper?"

"Because you have a small computer USB connector behind your ear, like Buddy and me. You escaped from Dr. Gore's lab too, didn't you?"

Molly lowered her head, "Shhhh. Yes, but the others don't know about that. If they did, they would be afraid to stay with me, just like they wanted to exile you and Buddy."

"How long will these men persist trying to find us?"

"Well, it's hard to say exactly, but they stopped looking for me after about three weeks."

"So if we can avoid capture for another week or two, they will probably give up or look elsewhere, right?"

"I don't think their leaders have much patience."

"Molly, how long ago did you escape and why?"

"Almost two years ago. Dr. Gore planned to operate on me to implant some new computer device in my brain. He had to wait for development of the device to be completed. I overheard him tell one of the scientists the operation was new and risky. He said the new device would be a breakthrough, if I didn't die from the procedure. A lab tech took me outside for a walk a few days after that. He let me off the leash to run around. I realized this was my opportunity to escape, so I ran down the hill, through the brush. I disappeared into the open-space forest, and fortunately, they never found me. I joined up with a few other stray dogs that have now become our pack."

"Was the lab tech named Sean?"

"No. And I'm sure they must have fired my lab tech for allowing me escape."

"Now I understand why Dr. Gore went so ballistic when our lab tech, Sean Keegan, let us off-leash outside one day. Dr. Gore is still operating on dogs, implanting his devices and experimenting with us in his laboratory. I hope someday we can stop him once and for all!"

"If we ever get the chance to bring Dr. Gore down, count me in!"

Molly and Pepper rejoined the pack, which sat spellbound, listening to Buddy's exaggerated tales of bravery and heroism of how he had led the NIA agents away from the pack.

12. Stair stares

Alex peeked into his backpack as he descended the stairs on his way to his next class. He saw his textbooks and homework inside, so he wouldn't have to go to his locker. Alex did not notice Bart Quisling climbing up the other side of the stairwell. Bart gave Alex a sharp poke with his elbow. Alex crashed into the railing and lost his balance. He bounced off the tiled wall and pitched forward Alex reached for the railing but missed on his first try. He clawed at the wall to stop his fall but still stumbled down a few steps. He finally grabbed the handrail, but collided with the girl, who was walking in front of him. The girl fell forward and turned her ankle with a pain filled "*OUCH*"

The girl's friend Meaghan reached out to stop Paige's fall. "Watch out Alex, you clumsy fool! Look what you have done!"

"But it wasn't my fault! Bart pushed me!"

Meaghan looked, but Bart was nowhere in sight. "He's not even on the stairs Alex."

"He was. It was Bart that caused all this. Honest."

Alex reached down to give Paige a hand up. They locked eyes. She was a new student and the most awesome girl Alex had ever seen. She had strawberry-blond hair, stunning brown eyes with green flecks that totally captured his gaze. Her smile had perfect, mega-bright white teeth, the kind only Hollywood stars and super-models flashed. Alex stared like a zombie.

Paige ignored Alex's outstretched hand. She simply stared, no glared back at Alex. Her fiery eyes, lovely arched eyebrows and plump, moist lips were pinched with anger and pain as Meaghan helped her to her feet.

"Are you all right Paige? Do you want to go to the nurse's office for some ice for your ankle?"

"Maybe that's a good idea, to stop the swelling."

Paige limped and winced painfully down the steps.

Alex's face flushed red with embarrassment. He was in despair but he felt like racing after her … so her name is Paige. He stifled saying, 'Nice meeting you Paige.' Alex watched as Paige, the limping angel disappeared around the corner into the hallway, like a beautiful mirage.

13. Buddy's big mistake

The pack's hunt for breakfast the next day was unsuccessful. No rabbits, no squirrels, not even a smelly skunk was available for their daily meal.

Molly said, "Buddy, that's the way it is living in the wild; we don't get to eat every day."

Buddy was not accustomed to missing a meal. His stomach grumbled. He was not happy about being so hungry.

He walked over to Pepper, "I don't like this starvation thing. I'm tired of wandering around the woods with an empty stomach, while we try to catch some unfortunate critter to eat."

"Well, Buddy you have to get used to it. There's no kibble out here."

"I don't plan to get used to starving, when there is plenty of food so nearby!"

"Nearby? What are you talking about Buddy?"

"Look, all we have to do is to go to the shopping mall. There are dumpsters behind every restaurant and grocery market spilling over with perfectly good food. We can sneak in, gorge ourselves and sneak back out."

"Buddy there are a lot of people at the shopping plaza who might see us and alert the men who are after us!"

"Not a chance. They don't even know anyone is looking for us. Besides, people are too slow to catch us."

Molly joined the conversation. "Buddy, your plan is too dangerous. Pepper is right about this."

Buddy shook his head and said, "I'm going! You two can stay here and starve if you want."

Buddy walked in the direction of the Novato Vintage Oaks Shopping Plaza.

Pepper shrugged, and said, "I better go with him to keep him out of trouble. We'll be back later."

Molly said, "Be careful." Her tail was not wagging.

Buddy and Pepper found their way back to the highway and followed it south toward the large shopping plaza on the eastern side of the highway. The ARI building loomed high on a hilltop on the western side of the road. The sight of the ARI lab caused the iMutts to cringe. They were frightened but wishfully thought, maybe if they didn't look at The ARI building, the ARI people would not see them.

Pepper said, "Let's find a restaurant dumpster, eat whatever we can find and get out of here."

"Stop worrying Pepper. We'll be fine. This will be easy."

They came to the shopping mall, which had three restaurants that backed up to the highway. There were garbage cans and dumpsters lined up behind them and some were so full they had garbage spilling onto the ground.

"Look at all that food! I know, I know. I'm a genius, right Pepper?"

Buddy raced through a hole in the fence straight toward the closest dumpster. Pepper followed at a much more dignified trot. They found several plastic bags with meat scraps inside. They gulped and swallowed the food at an amazingly rapid pace. Buddy did not even bother to chew most of the time. Their next course was a large portion of French fries with gravy, and some fried chicken. What a feast. They were so busy gorging themselves, they failed to notice the Animal Control truck that had parked around the corner.

The Animal Control Officer got out of his truck without making a sound. He left the door ajar and grabbed a long pole with a noose at the end. He hugged the wall of the building down-wind from the iMutts. He peeked around the corner as the two dogs busily rummaged through the dumpster for food. He cursed, because alone he would only be able to capture one of the strays. He opened the loop on the end of his pole, took a deep breath and raced toward the dumpster. Buddy and Pepper were so engaged in their food pig-out, they failed to notice the man until he was within a few steps. The man ran straight toward them.

Buddy yelled, "Let's run in different directions!"

"Okay, let's go."

Pepper veered left away from the approaching man, while Buddy ran to the right, and crossed in front of him. The man turned toward Buddy, because he was his best chance for a capture. The rope circled Buddy's neck. The man pulled hard on the rope to tighten the noose. Buddy fell to the ground, unable to move. Buddy saw Pepper escape through the hole in the fence. He was relieved for his sister's escape. Pepper watched helplessly as the man placed Buddy into a cage on the truck. The truck had a fancy logo decal on the door, but thankfully, not the dreaded NIA seal.

Pepper returned to the pack of strays in the open-space and told them what had happened.

Molly said, "It's not like we didn't warn him. I hope he gets a chance to escape."

The animal control officer took Buddy to the "Novato Animal Rescue Center" (NARC) and placed him in a holding pen inside the building. Buddy had no collar and no dog tags, so they recorded him as a stray "Rescue" dog, case number 1653. There he sat alone next to larger holding pens containing another twenty dogs. Buddy did not know what would happen to him next. He cowered in his cage alone and frightened. At least, he didn't see any scientists in white lab coats and no sign of Dr. Gore. Buddy thought, Maybe this place would be safe, for now.

He texted Pepper, *I'm OK. I'm in a cage at some place called 'NARC'. Stay where you are and I'll find a way out of here.*

"OK, Buddy. Escape if you can and you know where to find us."

14. Captive again

The following morning, a lady muzzled Buddy and took him from his cage on a leash to a small examination room. It had high-intensity lights in the ceiling that reminded him of Dr. Gore's surgery room. Buddy's heart sped up as he felt an increased sense of alarm. A door opened, and a woman in a blue lab coat entered with an assistant behind her.

The person holding Buddy's leash told the blue-coated woman, "This one is NARC case 1653. He was captured behind some restaurants at the Vintage Oaks Shopping Plaza yesterday. He has no collar or tags, so we registered him as a stray rescue dog."

The lady in the blue lab coat placed her hand on Buddy's head and petted him. "Don't be afraid. You are safe here. I am a veterinarian, and I need to examine you. We need to know if you are healthy and don't have diseases that could harm the other animals here."

Her soft voice soothed Buddy, and he relaxed a bit. The lady made medical observations about

Buddy, and her assistant wrote everything onto a clipboard chart.

"The specimen, case 1653, is a young mixed-breed dog between one and two years old. He looks to be a mixture of Lab, Pointer and some other breed, perhaps a Border collie."

They put Buddy on a scale and weighed him. "He weighs 65 pounds, and he seems to be healthy, even if a bit scruffy from being in the wild. He has no visible injuries."

The vet told Buddy, "I am going to remove your muzzle, so I can look at your teeth and gums and take a swab from your mouth for the lab. This is quick and won't hurt a bit. Please be a nice dog, so we don't have to sedate or restrain you."

Carol always amazed the assistant with her ability to calm and relax dogs. It seemed to her that the dogs could understand what she said. Little did she know that in this case, the dog understood everything. Carol petted Buddy's head. She released the strap on the muzzle, and removed it from Buddy's snout with a slow and gentle touch. Buddy licked her hand to make sure Carol knew everything would be OK.

Carol smiled and looked at his teeth and gums saying, "Your teeth and gums are very healthy. They show no signs of malnutrition or disease. You have not been in the wild for long, have you? He is probably lost, and we should check for any lost pet inquiries matching this dog's description."

The assistant took a few pictures. The flash startled Buddy. The vet told Buddy she was going to give him a vaccination. She said he would feel a little pain when she injected the needle into his thigh, but it would be quick. Before Buddy had time to think, the needle went in, the shot was injected, and it was over. Carol gave Buddy a treat and a pat on his head. When Buddy returned to his cage, fresh bowls of kibble and water waited for him.

Buddy thought, This NARC place may not so bad after all. At least I won't have to hunt every day to catch my meals!

Robert Healy

15. The Adoption

By Saturday morning, Buddy was bored of being confined to his cage all day. After the escape from ARI, he had become accustomed to running free with the pack in the forest. It seemed like the cage at NARC was not much different than being a prisoner in the ARI lab. Except at NARC, there was nothing to do all day but sit around totally bored. The once repetitive and tedious ARI language training sessions, now seemed like fun by comparison.

A small group of people walked into the holding pen room. The door opened inward, and all of the caged dogs jumped up and down and barked as the people walked toward the holding pens. A smiling, plump lady, whom Buddy had seen several times before, led the people over to the caged dogs. The group consisted of a boy around twelve years old, a younger girl who was around eight or nine and a woman, who was almost certainly their mother. The NARC woman pointed at certain dogs and whispered something to the lady. The mom looked at the dogs, nodded her head and asked the lady a few questions. The young girl rushed over to the cage containing the youngest puppies. Two of the puppies leaped up, barking in a high-pitched *yip, yip* and licked her finger as she poked it through the wire mesh. The young boy wandered in the direction of Buddy's cage.

"Alex, look at all the dogs carefully to decide which one we should adopt, because you are the birthday boy, and you get to choose."

Alex shrugged and muttered, "Whatev. I know, I know. I can handle this Mom."

Buddy thought … So his name is Alex, and he gets to choose.

Most of the dogs jumped up and down, barked, and pawed the front of their cages. They seemed desperate to get out … probably because they were. Alex looked at the blur of hysterical dogs; it was hard to focus on any one of them because they all acted so hyper. Alex noticed Buddy, who sat alone in his adjacent cage. Buddy looked straight at Alex. Their eyes met. Buddy walked toward Alex wagging his tail. He calmly sat, tilted his head and looked straight up at Alex.

Alex thought, This dog is sort of cool and he's not a little puppy. He's bigger, and athletic with a deep chest, strong shoulders. His fur is cool looking, mostly black with some brown highlights and I like his small floppy ears. He looks smart and his eyes sparkle.

Buddy stared at Alex, cocked his head, and wagged his tail again.

Alex thought … And this dog is so calm compared to the others. He wags his tail, so he's friendly, but he doesn't go all hyper jumping and crying like the other dogs.

Alex took out his cell phone to text his friend Zoo. As he did, he noticed that Buddy's right ear stood up. Buddy's "spyware" computer chip had captured Alex's cell phone number and that of the friend he was texting. Alex laughed because he thought Buddy looked funny with his one ear sticking up.

"Hey Zoo, I'm at NARC. We're here to adopt a dog for my birthday."

"Cool. What kind?"

Alex used his phone to take a picture of Buddy, and sent it to Zoo.

"Hey, he's awesome. Later dude."

Alex put his phone in his pocket. Buddy wagged his tail and smiled.

Alex muttered to himself, "Wow, did I see that dog smile? Can dogs smile?"

Buddy nodded his head in a "Yes-like" motion.

Alex blinked his eyes and thought, Get a grip Alex. That must have been a sheer coincidence.

Alex wandered back near his mom and was distracted by the other dogs. Savannah was still enthralled with the little puppies.

Alex's mom asked, "Well young man, have you made up your mind?"

"I'm not totally sure, mom. I thought I knew, but there are so many to choose from."

Alex's sister ran over. "Alex! Alex! Come over here and look at these adorable puppies. They are like so totally the sweetest dogs ever! And that cute little fluffy one is like so the cutest!"

Alex looked at the dog Savannah pointed at, and said, "Are you kidding? That one totally sucks! It's one of those little buggy-eyed ankle biters that barks *YAP, YAP, YIP, YIP* all day. Forget that!"

Savannah's head dropped, her shoulders slumped, and she sighed with disappointment.

Alex's cell phone buzzed in his pocket. He took a step away and looked at the screen. It was a new text message. He pulled up the message and glanced at the screen.

The message was from "AX275" and said: "*Alex, pick funny ear.*"

Alex wondered who sent it and then looked at Buddy, whose ear was pointed upward. Alex shook his head in wonder, and put his phone back into his pocket.

His Mom interrupted his thought. "Alex, take your time before you decide."

"I want the one over there," he said, pointing at Buddy.

"Are you sure Alex? You have to be certain."

Savannah became more animated pointing toward the young puppy cage.

Alex said, "He's definitely the one. He is like totally sick!"

"Uh, is that a good thing, Alex?"

"Oh yeah, Mom, totes."

Alex's Mom shook her head, and told the NARC lady which dog they wanted.

Buddy wagged his tail and barked *thank you*.

The NARC lady said, "It sure looks like there is some sort of special connection between these two. You are very lucky."

She opened the cage door, reached in and removed the NARC ID tag from Buddy's collar and told one of the attendants to get a travel cage ready.

"Okay, come with me and we'll take care of the paperwork. Congratulations young man!"

Savannah glanced back toward the puppy cage and looked down at the floor, her arms pressed tight to her side and her hands tight fisted, like she was going to cry.

They followed the NARC lady to her office. A half-dozen dog and cat statues and other stuffed animals sat on her desktop. She invited the family to be seated, while she signed onto her computer. A blank adoption form appeared on her computer screen. Alex looked around her office and was amazed by the profusion of animal pictures and pet calendars on the walls. The table under the window looked like a greenhouse with so many potted plants on it. The nameplate on her desk read "Daisy Goodflower," which seemed so appropriate.

Daisy cleared her throat, and said, "Let's begin. First, the dog's identity." She picked up the NARC ID tag from a desk piled high with papers and files. She glanced at the tag, which had case number 1653 printed on it.

A lady poked her head into Daisy's office as she prepared to type the case information. She asked if she should get an adoption kit from the storage closet.

Daisy was distracted, and said, "Yes, and please, and have Manuel get a large travel cage ready as well. Thanks."

Daisy tossed the disposable tag for case number 1653 into her trashcan. She typed 1563 into the "case number" field on the adoption form by mistake. She failed to realize her transposition error as she tabbed down to the next section of the form.

"I hope you won't mind, but we ask a lot of questions to make certain each family is right for adoption of one of our animals."

Then she asked a zillion questions and recorded the answers onto the computer form.

"What is your name?"

"Dana Logan."

"And is there a Mr. Logan?"

Mrs. Logan dropped her head. "Yes … err no. There was, but he recently passed away."

"Oh, I am so sorry. I uh…."

"Thank you. You see, he was killed by the terrorist bomb at the Boston Marathon, six months ago."

Daisy felt her face flush with embarrassment. She regretted asking what turned out to be such an awkward and painful question. "Oh my God. I'm so sorry. That was so horrible and such a shock. I don't know what to say."

Mrs. Logan responded, "Well you had no way of knowing, so let's move on, if that's OK."

"Right. Oh my. OK, what is your home phone number?"

"Where do you live?"

"Do you have a backyard?"

"Is it fenced?"

"Do you have any other pets?"

"Have you had a dog before?"

"Have you ever adopted an animal before?"

"Have any of the children been bitten by a dog?"

"Do the children have any pet allergies?"

The questions continued for another ten minutes, until Daisy clapped her hands and proclaimed, "Thank heavens that's done! Now for the fun part."

Daisy gave Mrs. Logan all kinds of free doggy items, a bag of dog food, a few stuffed toys, a bag of dog treats, a leash and some other things they would need. Miss Goodflower explained the dog had been given his shots, had previously been neutered and also had a "doggie ID" chip implanted in his ear that could be scanned to identify him, if he ever became lost.

"The chip will enable any animal shelter to identify your dog and inform you where and how to pick him up."

Daisy gave Mrs. Logan her business card with her contact information in case there were any questions or problems later. Mrs. Logan wrote a check and left for the car with her bag of doggy booty.

"Congratulations again young man and young lady. Take good care of your new friend."

16. Going home

A man from NARC placed Buddy into a travel carrier and wheeled him out to Mrs. Logan's SUV. They opened the back hatch-door and he placed the cage into the cargo area. As Mrs. Logan closed the cargo door, Buddy noticed two men in suits emerge from a black sedan with an NIA sticker in the window. Buddy ducked down out of sight as both men glanced over at the Logan's SUV. The men walked into the NARC lobby, flashed their IDs to the receptionist. Ms. Goodflower rushed over, to see what they wanted. They disappeared into her office. Buddy suspected they were NIA agents, probably looking for him and Pepper. He hoped Alex's Mom would leave the parking lot quickly.

Alex was excited and wanted to sit next to the dog on the ride home. Mrs. Logan told him to get into the back seat and buckle up. Alex thought the dog seemed as amped as him. Alex and Savannah talked to the dog all the way home, so he wouldn't be scared. Buddy looked at them, tilted his head, as if he understood what they said. Then he curled up on the blanket and fell asleep.

Mrs. Logan maneuvered her SUV into their garage. Buddy awoke with a jolt, when Mrs. Logan hit the button for the garage door remote. The door rumbled and squeaked as it closed and thumped to a stop. Alex told Buddy not to worry. Mrs. Logan opened the door of the dog carrier and Buddy jumped onto the garage floor. Mrs. Logan carried the empty dog carrier to the kitchen and placed it on the tile floor. She placed bowls for food and water on two carpet tiles in the laundry room.   She cleared a space under a table near the washer/drier and placed the dog carrier under the table. Mrs. Logan said, "I want the dog to sleep in the laundry room in this travel carrier. It will be his indoor doghouse. I'll have a pet door installed, so he'll have access to the back yard."

Neither Alex nor Savannah thought having the dog sleep in the laundry room was a great idea.

17. The hunt continues

Unknown to the Logan family, the two NIA agents in the NARC parking lot spoke to Daisy Goodflower, about two dogs that had escaped from a nearby high-security government laboratory. The men gave Daisy their business cards with their contact information. She scrutinized their business cards and was surprised they were from NIA, the National Intelligence Agency. One of the men was Deputy Les Smart and the other was Agent Mason Dixon.

Les Smart said she should be on the lookout for the two escaped dogs and to contact them immediately if they turned up at NARC. The dogs were special and had been trained for sensitive counter terrorism work. He handed her two small photographs. Daisy placed them face down on her desktop while she continued to glance at the business cards.

Agent Mason Dixon told her to report anything unusual. But when Daisy asked, "Like what?" he could not explain what he meant.

They asked her to show them the dogs currently held at the NARC facility. Miss Goodflower gave them a tour of the dog holding area. None of the dogs fit the description of the runaways.

Deputy Les Smart asked, "What about the dog we saw in the parking lot when we arrived?"

"That dog was adopted by a lovely family. I'll show you the paperwork."

She took the agents back to her office and retrieved the printout of the Logan's adoption papers from her desktop.

"Yes, here it is," she muttered, "He was case number 1563. We keep meticulous records of all of our animals," she said raising her head with pride.

"When did you say the two dogs you are looking for escaped from the lab?"

Les Smart glanced at his paperwork and said, "A little over two weeks ago."

Miss Goodflower typed in case number 1563 into her computer and the case file appeared on her computer screen. She pointed to her LCD screen and said, "Well the dog you saw in the parking lot was case number 1563. He was brought to this shelter six weeks ago, so it could not be one of the dogs you are looking for."

Agent, Mason Dixon looked at the screen for confirmation and nodded. Ms. Goodflower closed the file. The computer wallpaper picture of her five cats reappeared on her screen. She waived the printout of the official-looking adoption papers at them and placed them in her file drawer.

The computer record for case number 1653 would have shown that the dog had been brought to the shelter only three days ago, and exactly two weeks after the dogs had escaped from the ARI laboratory.

The agents nodded, thanked her for her time and rose to leave. They exited the front door, went to their car and headed to the next animal rescue shelter on their list.

Agent Les Smart grumbled, "When I signed up to be with the intelligence agency, I didn't think I would be hunting for lost dogs!"

18. Name that puppy

The following morning, Savannah and Alex fed the dog. His tail wagged happily. Everyone relaxed after breakfast and was amused by the antics of their brand-new family addition.

Mrs. Logan said, "What shall we name him?"

Savannah said, "How about Fluffy?"

She was still thinking about the fluffy puppies she had hoped they would adopt. Nobody responded to her suggestion. Alex thought … How lame is Fluffy, our dog has short hair.

Mrs. Logan said, "Alex, perhaps you should come up with a name, since the dog was your birthday present."

Alex thought hard. All I have to do is to come up with a name one other person likes and nobody totally trashes as dorky, like Fluffy. The harder Alex tried, the more his mind became a complete blank. After a while, he was not even sure he could remember his own name. Mrs. Logan and Savannah stared at him, expecting him to say something brilliant. The tension mounted.

Alex thought, Man, I'm feeling the pressure but it's nothing to get flamed about. I can do this. Think, Alex, think! His smart-phone vibrated in his pocket. He had a new text message. The message was from the mysterious "AX275," and said, "*Alex, my name is Buddy.*"

Alex texted back, "*Who is this?*"

"*Somebody who knows his own name!*"

Alex thought, What's going on here? Who is sending me these weird text messages?

Alex pondered a few more seconds, and said, "I think his name should be Buddy."

"Why would you think that, Alex?" his mom asked.

"Call it a hunch, Mom. I think his name is Buddy."

Buddy jumped up and down and barked enthusiastically.

Mrs. Logan said, "My goodness, the dog seems to like the name Buddy. I think Buddy is a cute name too. Okay Alex, Buddy is it."

Buddy wagged his tail, sneezed and then barked with what seemed to be a happy note.

Everyone called to Buddy. "Hey Buddy, come here, Buddy … Buddy, your name is Buddy. … Do you like Buddy?"

Buddy wondered what all the fuss was, and thought, sometimes people were strange. He walked over to his food bowl for a bite of kibble.

Mrs. Logan took out her cell phone to make a call. As she did, Alex saw Buddy's ear pointed straight up, like at the rescue center when Alex had texted his friend, Zoo. It was as if Buddy was about to listen to the phone call. Mrs. Logan changed her mind and put the phone in her pocket. Buddy's ear dropped back down.

Alex thought, This must be my imagination, probably nothing, chillax.

Still, Alex wondered where those AX 275 text messages had come from?

Robert Healy

19. Not your ordinary dog

"Okay Alex, Buddy has a name, now go take care of your homework. You've had a big weekend, but you can't neglect your schoolwork, so get going!"

Mrs. Logan gently guided Alex upstairs to his room and over to his desk. She handed him his backpack. "Here you go. Get started."

Buddy jumped onto Alex's bed, turned around three times to make a nest, and flopped down. Alex had already restarted "Dark Star Warrior" which flashed up on the screen.

"No, no, no Alex. No games until your homework is done. Shut that down!"

"Mom, why do I have to do these stupid math problems? It seems to me the only use for algebra and stuff is if I became a math teacher. Then I would have to force another generation of students to do useless math problems."

"Alex, you're too young to understand why math homework is important."

"Oh yeah! Once I asked dad when was the last time he had to solve a word problem in his job? And dad is, uhhhmm, was a very successful business executive."

Alex choked up, but tried to hide his emotions. "And dad said, 'Well, uhh never, I guess.' Sooo, what is the point of doing all this math stuff? It's boring and a waste of time, too."

"It's not a waste of time, Alex. Math teaches you how to think about and solve problems. When you go to college, if you decide to be a scientist or engineer, you will need to use math everyday."

Then his mom added with a tone of finality, "That's why!"

Alex thought, It's probably pointless to try to persuade mom to let me skip math homework. I might as well get it over with, so I can get back to Dark Star and crush Zygor, the Evil Emperor.

"Get cracking young man!" And then she left.

Alex had only finished two of the ten assigned math problems, when his mind started to wander back to the game. He grabbed the game controller and clicked *resume.* The game restarted where he had left off. Alex's Mom peeked in his door, as Alex restarted level six on Mortu, where the swamp creature had killed him.

"Alex what are you doing? Turn the game off, NOW!"

"Hey! How about some privacy? Shouldn't you knock first?"

"Apparently you need someone looking over your shoulder every minute, young man!"

"I'll get my homework done. I don't need you all over my case! Dad wouldn't hassle me over this. He understood me better than you, and he trusted me. You don't understand anything. I wish dad were here! He would …" Alex burst into tears.

Mom rushed over to him and hugged him, "Oh Alex, it's OK to cry. Let it out. I miss your father too and I'm angry with those evil terrorists who took him from us. I know it's so painful now and hard to understand."

"Mom, it will always be painful! And what's to understand? Why did he have to run in that stupid race? Why did those loser guys want to kill innocent people anyway? Why did Dad have to be right where the bomb blew up? I want my dad back!"

"We all want him back, but that can't happen. We have to deal with what is and keep on living somehow. And we have to support each other, and always remember how wonderful he was to us."

"I've tried mom, but it's hard and I'm so angry. Why did this happen to us?"

Alex's mom gave him another hug, kissed the top of his head and said, "That's the way life is. I know you are having a hard time with this. You are angry, and that's normal. Your schoolwork has slipped which is not like you. But we must all work together to get you back on track. It's what your dad would want. Come on, we have to get back to normal even if it doesn't feel like normal."

"OK Mom I'll try. Thanks."

"Now, please get back to your homework. It's part of 'normal,' Alex." His Mom gave him another hug, a big smile and left his room again.

Alex wasn't ready to restart his math homework after all the emotion that had welled up. He saved his Dark Star Warrior game, shut down the computer and flopped onto his bed trying to get his act together.

Alex's Smart-Phone buzzed in his pocket.

"Now, what?"

Alex pulled up his text message screen. It was another message from the mysterious AX275.

"*Alex, you are right to feel angry and confused about your dad's death. Your mom loves you, and she was right about having to work through this. Let me try to help too. I know what it's like to have your whole world turned upside down too. Buddy.*"

Alex texted back, "*Who the heck are you, how did you get my text address and what do you want?*"

Seconds later he received a response,

"*I already told you, I'm Buddy. Remember when I texted you at NARC, and then you picked me. And when you tried to think up a name, I told you my name was Buddy. I just want to help. By the way, I understand English, so you can talk to me…. It's easier. I have to text you because I can't speak. OK?*"

Alex looked at Buddy and said, "Oh come on. How stupid do you think I am? Dogs can't text!"

"*Well, this one can and so can my sister Pepper. We're special dogs.*"

"OK. If you are the "so special" one who texted me, sneeze twice, right now."

Buddy looked up at Alex and sneezed twice. Alex was shocked.

That had to be a lucky coincidence. "OK, send me a text that says, my name is Buddy."

Alex received a text within seconds, "*My name is Buddy. Convinced ye*t?"

"Yes, I mean NO! This is cray-cray dude! How can you do this?"

"*It's a long story, Alex.*"

Buddy sent Alex several lengthy text messages. He told Alex about Dr. Seymour Gore, the lab, the implanted computers, brain wave scanner, the genetic engineering, the language training for being an NIA "spy-dog". He told him about the meeting with NIA and how Dr. Gore planned to perform a life threatening operation on him and his sister, Pepper. Then he described their daring escape, with the help of Sean Keegan.

Alex asked frequent questions. He tried to comprehend what he had learned about his no longer ordinary dog. Buddy told him about the NIA secret agents who were searching for Pepper and him and that if they were recaptured, they would probably be killed. Buddy told him their entire conversation had to remain their secret.

"*Alex, nobody can know who I really am, not even your Mom.*"

Alex understood and agreed. "But this is going to be a difficult secret to keep."

Sensing Alex's concern, Buddy texted, "*My secret and my life are in your hands. I trust you.*"

Alex reached out, hugged Buddy and said, "Buddy, you are so totally awesome. I won't even tell my Mom! Dude, we have so much stuff to talk about."

"*There will be plenty of time for that later. Right now get the math homework done before your mom comes back. I can't help you with that because I'm lousy at math.*"

Buddy then texted Pepper, "*I am OK. I'm no longer at NARC. A family that needs me right now has adopted me. I may stay here awhile. Text me when you can.*"

Every afternoon after school, Alex took Buddy for a walk to a nearby park. Alex let Buddy off-leash, so they could play ball. Alex tried to teach Buddy to catch a Frisbee, but that was going to take some serious hard work. After they returned home, they went up to Alex's room and "chatted" for an hour or more. At first, Alex wanted to know everything about Buddy and Pepper, their lives at the lab and their escape.

After a while, the chats became more about what was on Alex's mind. In a matter of days, Buddy became Alex's best friend and favorite advisor. Alex was grateful to have someone he could trust and talk to about his dad, school and other issues. Buddy felt like he had an important job to do as Alex's best friend. Buddy thought, At last I have found what's been missing … a purpose.

20. The new girl in town

Monday soon arrived, and it was back to school at Chester A. Arthur Middle School. Alex wondered why his school was named after one of the most obscure presidents ever. President Arthur accomplished almost nothing during his one term. He had a reputation for being a snappy dresser and a good fisherman … not exactly history-making praise for a U.S. President. Alex rushed into his homeroom a little late, with his backpack dangling from his hand. As Alex strode across the front of the classroom, he spotted the new girl. Paige sat like a goddess in the third row. There was something about her that excited him but also made him feel a bit nervous and shy at the same time.

Alex had begun to notice girls for reasons he was unable to explain. They seemed different now in a curious and nice way. Not that he would ever want to spend a lot of time with girls, but still there was suddenly something interesting and mysterious about them … and Paige in particular. Alex thought, Most girls think video games, computers and sports are dumb, so what would I talk with them about? But this girl Paige seemed unusually attractive, in an almost irresistible way.

Bart Quisling sat in the front row and stuck out his foot as Alex passed by. Alex tripped and lurched forward out of control. His arms flapped, and his backpack and pencils arched through the air and landed on top of the teacher's desk. The soaring backpack sent her desk calendar and papers flying. The entire class erupted in laughter. Alex looked like a complete klutz, scrambling on the floor to retrieve his stuff.

Quisling mocked Alex, "Have a nice trip Alex?"

Mrs. Langley interrupted the laughter, and said, "Alex, can you please take your seat now?"

Alex felt a warm flush of embarrassment, as he slumped toward his desk amidst the cascade of snickers from everywhere in the room.

Alex looked over at Paige, but she looked away and down at her desktop, as if it was somehow extremely interesting … more interesting than Alex, apparently.

Alex fumed in silence and thought, Oh great! Now I'm the class klutz and have probably already blown what chances I may have had with Paige! She won't want anything to do with me after the fall on the stairwell and now this. All because of that idiot Bart Quisling!

Alex's Mom sometimes asked him, "Why aren't you friends with Bart Quisling? He plays sports, and his Mom and Dad are such nice people."

Alex thought, Mom doesn't realize Bart is bad news. He always causes trouble and he loves to bully other kids. All of his friends are losers with bad grades, and he's constantly getting into trouble. Alex wouldn't be surprised if Bart grew up to become a psycho criminal. You know, the kind of goon that on TV News broadcasts, was being handcuffed and taken away to jail by the police for robbing a bank or shooting someone. Reporters would be flashing pictures and screaming questions like, "Bart, are you sorry you did it?" And Bart would snarl, "No, just sorry I got caught! Now get lost!"

Some kids at school thought Bart was the one who threw stones off the overpass into the highway traffic, but there was no proof. Alex knew Bart bumped into people in the hallways and stairs between classes, because he had done it to him twice. But nobody ever said anything, because they were afraid of what Bart might do to a squealer. Alex avoided Bart as much as possible.

At lunchtime Alex said "Hi" to Paige in the hallway. She did not seem to notice him. She glided by with those beautiful brown eyes locked straight ahead; while she stirred the air with what Alex thought was electricity.

Alex's friend, Jo smiled and said, "Looks like you made a real great impression on her, Alex."

"Yeah, Jo, she's crazy about me… NOT! But, she did notice me today in homeroom, as I crawled on the floor to pick up all my stuff, after Bart the dork tripped me. I hope she is attracted to klutzes, in which case I'll be her number one prospect."

Jo thought, LOL! It looks like Alex is in love!

Jo, who's real name was Jose, was one of Alex's best friends. His family came to the US from Peru about five years ago. Jo spoke English and Spanish, which came in handy at times … like when Alex and his friends met a Spanish-speaking family that was on vacation from Puerto Rico, and became lost. They were so happy to get help from Jo.

At real Mexican restaurants, Jo knew exactly how to order what everybody wanted. But once Jo ordered extra hot habanero sauce for Alex's burrito.

Alex had a rude surprise and yelled, "Dude, this is SO HOT!"

He gulped down three glasses of water, which only seemed to make things worse. Everybody laughed, while Alex gasped. But, that joke aside, Jo was usually a good guy. Jo felt bad about the prank afterward and said he was sorry. But Alex thought it was pretty funny too, in retrospect.

Girls thought Jo was so cute because he looked like some sort of Spanish TV star. You know, the kind with dark penetrating eyes, high cheekbones, a bit of swagger and a devilish 'bad boy' smile. And all the girls thought he had a cute accent. Jo always seemed to know what to say to girls. And whatever he said, the girls giggled and sighed. When Alex tried to act cute like Jo, the girls said, "Get lost Alex" and kept on walking. Alex didn't get it, but he watched everything Jo did and said. He hoped someday to figure out Jo's secrets, so maybe even Paige would notice him too.

That night, after he finished his homework, Alex told Buddy about Paige.

"Buddy she's totally awesome. I think she might be a Royal Princess, who wanted to go to public school to meet real people, you know, like undercover or something."

"Alex, all you have talked about since you arrived home has been Paige this and Paige that. I'm making a wild guess you like this girl."

"Yeah. But she doesn't seem interested in me. I guess I'll have to do something spectacular to attract her attention, huh?"

"What, you mean, like make a fool of yourself or something?"

"No Buddy, I've already done that. You know, like do something totally cool or something."

"I don't know much about girls, but if Paige is anything like my sister, Pepper, she won't be impressed with any, 'Oh, look at me' sort of antics."

"All right, so what would you do, Mr. I'm so the smartest dog in the world?"

"Well, for starters, 'Mr. I haven't got a clue,' I would not try too hard or show too much interest, because it freaks people out. And besides, most people seem to want what they can't have. So act like you're not so interested in her. Don't be negative, be

nice, but be cool. Act like, you're nice Paige, but there are a lot of other fish in the sea. She'll begin to wonder why you're not falling for just her. Then she'll think all the other girls must be nuts about you, and that you can have your pick. Then she'll decide to try to somehow attract your attention. And Bingo! Advantage Alex."

"But Buddy, Paige IS super-special and all the girls AREN'T nuts about me. How could that lame strategy ever work?"

"Because, there's only one thing that matters. It's all about what people perceive, not what is actually real. Look at your friend Jo. Is he really different or do the girls simply THINK he's special?"

"Do you mean I should act like Jo?"

"No, just be you. People like people who have confidence in themselves. Relax, be yourself and don't try too hard. That's my advice."

"OK. I guess it's worth a shot. I couldn't do any worse than I am now."

Robert Healy

21. Alex gets busted

Mrs. Langley gave the class an assignment to do a report about a famous person; someone who invented something important or who had made lives better for sick or disadvantaged people. Usually the boys chose someone like LeBron James, Dr. Martin Luther King or Derek Jeter for their reports. Alex decided to be different and do a report on Nikola Tesla. Tesla invented the concept of alternating electrical current (AC), which enabled electricity to be delivered long distances over power lines. AC was the kind of electricity service delivered to everybody's home today.

Alex thought, What kind of world it would be with no electrical service at home? We'd be living in the dark ages; with no computers, no cell phones, no game consoles and no HD TV. Instead of watching reality shows on TV, we'd just have reality. People would be forced to communicate with only face-to-face conversations and we'd have to read books for entertainment. Tesla had to be one of the most important people in history, but almost nobody knew much about him, because he was such an eccentric nerd.

Tesla had invented some totally cool stuff, but because he was a major tech-weenie, cooler people like Edison got all the credit. Alex went onto the Internet to do more Tesla research. He searched for the name, "Nikola Tesla". *Wham*, an instant list of website information categories about Tesla appeared, with everything you ever wanted to know about him: Tesla quotes, biographies, theory of free energy, the death ray (*wow*), inventions, time travel (*wow again*) and patents appeared. Alex selected biographies to start and up popped several pages of website links to choose from.

Alex wondered about how kids did reports like this before the Internet. He imagined how kids went to a library and read through a stack of books. They had to hand-write notes about everything of interest that they read on their topic. Then they would go home and rewrite the information from their notes into a report. If they made a mistake or left something out, they would have to either correct it by hand, or maybe even rewrite the whole report.

What a drag, he thought. With computers, I can copy and paste the information from a website into my "*tesla_report.doc*." Then Alex wondered if instead of Tesla, he should do his report on whoever had invented "copy and paste". After all, their supersized idea had certainly made life better for him and millions of other kids, who had to write reports for school.

Alex selected two websites that had everything he needed for his Tesla report. He highlighted the sections he wanted for the report, copied and then pasted them into his *tesla_report.doc*.

Sweet! This report is totally epic, if I must say so myself. He thought, Mrs. Langley will be totally impressed with this report, an instant A+.

With his report done, Alex moved on to more important things, like playing video games. Alex knew this was not the way he was supposed to do the report, but it was so fast, so easy not to mention mega-cool.

The day after Alex handed in his report, Mrs. Langley kept him after class. Alex figured she would tell him what a great report it was, and maybe ask him to read it to the class as an example of how reports should be done. Mrs. Langley congratulated him for choosing an important and often overlooked person as Nikola Tesla for his report.

She asked, "Alex, are you interested in electrical engineering or science as a career?"

Alex said, "It seems pretty cool, particularly Tesla's death ray and time travel research. They are like totally swag."

Mrs. Langley said, "Your report is very well written and so informative."

Alex thanked her and said, "I worked hard on the research."

Big mistake! Mrs. Langley explained how she had done a web-search on some of the sentences in his report, for example: *"In his early research, Tesla devised several experimental setups to produce X-rays."* She pretended surprise that the search led her directly to the Wikipedia report about Nikola Tesla.

"Alex, by a strange coincidence, the Wikipedia article was the same, word for word, as most of your report."

Alex lamely suggested that perhaps he should take some kind of legal action against Wikipedia for copying his report and posting it on-line without his permission.

Mrs. Langley cut short an involuntary laugh, stared at Alex with her hands on her hips and a stern look of disapproval on her face. Then Mrs. Langley gave Alex a strong lecture about plagiarism, and the almost life threatening consequences for students caught using such dishonest practices. First, Alex would receive an 'F' for the report. Next she would have to inform his mom that her darling boy had cheated and his school record would forever reveal the details of his crime. That would be followed by possible suspension from school. A dark cloud of dishonesty would follow him the rest of his life.

Alex thought, "Well perhaps I could still become a politician or lawyer, because honesty is optional in those fields."

Alex was almost about to give up hope, when Mrs. Langley said, "But since this is your first offense Alex, perhaps there is room for a more lenient solution to this problem. But this will only be possible if you promise me you will never plagiarize again, and to accept your punishment."

"Of course" Alex said, "Anything Mrs. Langley, I'm sorry, my bad and I promise to never do it again. Please don't tell my Mom, (blah, blah, blah), please."

Mrs. Langley pondered silently, while Alex freaked-out inside. He watched his life flash before his eyes. Alex saw himself wandering the streets as an orphan, disowned by his family, dumpster diving for food and eating at soup kitchens with scary people.

Then Mrs. Langley broke her silence. "Here is what we will do. I'll agree to keep this incident between the two of us, if you agree to write two new reports. They must be properly researched, properly footnoted for sources, and on my desk no later than Monday. Make one report about a famous man and the other about an equally famous woman. Oh and Alex, let's make them a minimum of five pages each. Do you agree?"

What could Alex say, No I'd rather be orphaned and descend into a world of crime, living on the streets? So Alex responded, "OK, but how about, due next Wednesday and could you make it four pages each?"

Mrs. Langley wrinkled her brow with a look of surprise and muttered "What?"

She looked at Alex astonished, like he had just arrived from another planet. She then put her hands on her hips, tilted her head, smiled and said; "OK Mr. Smarty, let's make that six pages each and still due on Monday. Take it or leave it Alex. When you get caught cheating 'red handed', you are not in a position to negotiate better terms. I hope you enjoy the weekend Alex."

Alex figured this new report assignment would cancel his fun weekend plans, but what choice did he have?

So Alex meekly said, "OK Mrs. Langley. And I am sorry."

Alex wondered briefly, What the heck did getting caught "red handed" actually mean anyway?

Mrs. Langley said, "All will be forgiven, Alex. Make sure the reports are well-done, HONEST efforts and on my desk Monday morning! Be sure to credit your sources at the end."

Later at home, Alex sat at his computer doing research for his two reports. First he searched the web for the phrase "Getting caught red handed." He found what he was looking for at a website called, "Origins of idiomatic expressions." These are expressions that, while we learn what the phrases mean, the words don't always seem to make much literal sense. There are lots of these expressions that sometimes date back hundreds of years to farming, military or seafaring origins. Alex found one popular explanation for the origin of 'getting caught red handed". It referred to catching a murderer with the victim's blood still on their hands. *UHGG*, Alex was sorry he had checked that one out.

Buddy wandered into the Alex's room, his tail happily wagging, as usual.

"Alex, what are you working on?"

"Oh I have to do two lame reports on famous people for Mrs. Langley!"

"I thought you already did one, about Nikola Tesla."

"Yeah but Mrs. Langley went all neg on me. She said I so cheated, because I had copied and pasted stuff from Wikipedia into the report."

"But you knew it was cheating when you did it, right?"

"Well, sort of. OK yeah I knew it wasn't right. So now I have to do two reports for punishment!"

"Sounds like she let you off easy. After all she didn't tell your mom or flunk you. You should be thankful for that."

"Yeah, I guess. Mom would have gone ballistic. Hey Buddy, why don't you help me out and do one of the reports for me?"

Buddy smiled, turned and left the room.

On Monday Alex gave Mrs. Langley two reports; one on Dr. Jonas Salk, the inventor of the polio vaccine and the other on Florence Nightingale, the famous nurse, author and statistician. He figured she had to be impressed with reports about people who saved thousands of lives. In a way, Mrs. Langley saved his life by not reporting him, but Alex had learned his lesson the hard way.

Alex told his friend Jo about what had happened. Jo told Alex the problem was that he had gotten caught. He suggested the Alex had to be cleverer and copy from more sources in the future. Alex thought, Jo had so missed the whole point about the importance of being honest in the first place.

Robert Healy

22. Trouble finds Paige

After Alex handed in his reports, he left Mrs. Langley's classroom to go home. He stopped at his locker to get schoolbooks for his homework assignments and noticed Paige, nearby.

"Hey Paige, how's your campaign for student council president going?"

Then Alex noticed Paige was crying and he asked, "What's wrong Paige?"

Paige responded, "Oh nothing, nothing at all."

"You're in the hallway crying but nothing is wrong. That's so not believable."

"It's something personal, and you don't need to get involved with it."

"But Paige, maybe I can help?"

"I don't think there is anything you can do Alex."

"You never know Paige, try me!"

"OK. Somebody trashed my campaign posters. Look at this!"

Paige showed Alex one of her posters. Pasted under her name was a sticker that said "**Is A Goofy Dweed.**" It covered up the words "For Student Council President."

"And I worked so hard to make these posters. It's not fair!"

"Can't you just peel the stickers off?"

"No, I tried that, but the glue is too strong and it ruins them. And I don't have time to make them all over again and the election is next week!"

"How about if I help you? Maybe we can print "For Student Council President" labels and paste them over these "Is A Goofy Dweed" stickers. I can print them out this afternoon. I can fix the posters and we'll replace them in the morning. How does that sound?"

"It's a great idea, Alex. You are so clever. But what if they ruin the posters again?"

Alex blushed. "They may try, but maybe we can catch them, red handed."

"But how can we do that, Alex?"

"I'm working on it."

"But Alex, there's more. Somebody has posted nasty and untrue comments about me on the Blahblahbook social media website using an alias 'The Exposer.' They even posted a picture of me in my underwear, changing for gym class. I have no idea who would do such an evil thing to me. But, if this continues, I'll be the laughing stock of the school. It's so embarrassing and I'll never get elected Student Council President!"

"Paige, it must be a girl in your gym class because the photo was taken in the girl's locker room. It might even be the same person trashing your campaign posters."

"You're right, but I have no idea who this 'Exposer' is. I am so angry, but I don't know what I can do!"

"As the class techno-geek, I know it's not easy to figure out who is bullying you on social media sites when they post using an alias. We need to trace the true identity of the person who made the posting. I might know someone who can help us."

"Who, Alex. Who can do that?"

"Better you don't know the details, trust me. If I'm right, we'll know the culprit is pretty soon.

And I think I know how we can catch the person who defaced your posters too!"

"If you can find out who is doing these things to me and stop them it would be the greatest thing ever!"

That was all Alex needed to hear. He had already put a plan together in his mind.

23. To catch a cyber-bully

When he got home, Alex raced straight up to his room to see if Buddy could help resolve Paige's problem.

"Buddy, I know your spyware programs can capture contact directories for cell phones and e-mails, but can you trace the identity of people who use an alias to make posts in Blahblahbook or Tweety?"

"Maybe, but why do you want to know that?"

Alex explained Paige's problem of the cyber-bully Blahblahbook postings and how her campaign posters had been vandalized.

"I hoped we, uh or that is you could help uncover the cyber-bully. Can you?"

"Probably, but first I need to know Paige's Blahblahbook page address, so I can capture and download all of her Blahblah Friends' addresses."

"No problem. It's, Blahblahbook.com/paige.madison

"Great. I'll use my "Ping" program. It sends a secret 'spy-code' message to all the people who

have posted on Paige's Blahblah page, and returns their computer IP addresses to me. When I get answers to all of the Pings, I can compare the addresses to see if any of them match the mystery Exposer's IP address. If we get a match, we'll catch the cyber-bully. It's quite simple actually."

"Buddy you are totally awesome. If we can catch the bully, Paige will think I am the greatest!"

"Alex, what about the campaign poster vandal? They may be the same person, but do you have a plan to catch them?"

"Yes, I do. Leave that one to me. I'll be right back!"

Alex opened the door to his bedroom closet and turned the light on. It was a large closet and with a small access opening in the back, which led into a storage area above the garage. Alex used this area as a secret place to hide lots of things his mom might otherwise suggest he throw away. Alex grabbed his flashlight and crawled through the access door into the storage space. The dusty floor caused Alex to sneeze. He froze, hoping his Mom had not heard him. She didn't know about his secret hiding place. He heard nothing but silence, so Alex moved forward, careful to avoid knocking over any boxes.

He knew what box he wanted. It was the carton filled with assorted electronic gadgets.

Alex moved a few cartons so he could get to the rear-most boxes. With the help of a flashlight, Alex spotted the box with the words "electronic stuff" scribbled on the side. Alex dragged the box forward, opened the lid and peered inside. He found his miniature motion sensor activated Spy-Cam XL-15, right near the top of the carton. It was tiny, about the size of a small candy bar and was powered by one AAA battery. A motion sensor activated the camera and it could record up to 400 still pictures or up to 20 thirty-second video segments, before running out of memory. Alex grabbed the spy cam, closed the carton and returned to his bedroom. He had purchased the spy cam at an electronics swap for $20. Usually this type of surveillance camera sold for around $95. Alex remembered how cool he thought the Spy-Cam was, when he bought it. Now it would be used in the most important way Alex could imagine.

"Hey Buddy, check this out. You're not the only super spy here. Pretty cool huh?"

"Yeah, way cool. What is it?"

"OMG you're supposed to be a spy-dog and you don't even know what a 'Spy-Cam XL-15' is? LOL"

"Well, it looks sort of primitive. I on the other hand, am a living, breathing spy-cam. And much better, I'd say. And I don't need batteries."

"Well, this has a motion sensor and it takes surveillance pictures and videos. So Buddy, with any luck, I think we'll catch the poster vandal in the act with my Spy-Cam."

Alex put a fresh battery into the device and placed it into his backpack along with a screwdriver and some duct tape.

"Now for those campaign posters."

Alex measured the size of the "Is A Goofy Dweed" stickers that were on the posters. He formatted a replacement sticker that said, "For Student Council President." Alex printed the new stickers on the heavy photo paper. They looked great! Alex trimmed the four new stickers to exact size and pasted them on top of the "Is A Goofy Dweed" stickers. He used Gorilla glue, so by morning, the new stickers could not be peeled off.

The next day he met Paige at school 30 minutes before classes. Paige was amazed at how good the posters looked with Alex's repair job. Paige threw her arms around Alex and gave him a big hug and a kiss. Alex felt his face get a bit warm as he staggered back not knowing what to do.

He became flustered and stammered something about "We have work to do. You take the posters and place them where you want them. But we'll put one on the bulletin board across from my locker before you go. I'll see you later at homeroom."

Paige placed her campaign poster on the bulletin board across from Alex's locker and hurried down the hall to put up the other three posters elsewhere. Alex opened his locker, loosened two screws and removed the metal plate with his locker number engraved upon it. The steel locker number plate had covered a small round hole in the locker door. Alex taped the Spy-Cam to the inside of the locker door so the camera lens and motion sensor peeked out through the hole in the door. Alex turned the device on, set it to 20-second video mode and closed his locker door. He walked over to the bulletin board to test the device, as if he was going to post something. Then Alex reopened his locker and connected the Spy-Cam to his laptop. He opened the Spy-Cam app and played the video of him walking up to the bulletin board.

Alex thought, "OMG that is so clear. Much better than I expected! I wonder if there are any school rules against this? Well, I guess I'll worry about that after we catch the campaign poster vandal." Alex reset the Spy-Cam device and walked to his homeroom.

At the end of classes that day, Alex checked the spy-cam. There were lots of short videos, but none showing a poster vandal. Alex reset the spy-cam and went home. That evening Alex and Buddy had their usual chat, but much later than usual, because Alex had to study for a test. Buddy's had rules, like No chats until Alex's finished his homework!

Alex closed his schoolbooks, his homework done!

"Buddy, I'm set up to bust the poster vandal. Have you made any progress with the cyber-bully?"

"You could say so."

"Don't tease me Buddy. What did you find out?"

"It turned out that, 'The Exposer' had the same computer IP address as another Blahblahbook "friend" named Charlene Gump. Does that make any sense?"

"Like a total bull's-eye dude. This is HUGE! Charlene is running against Paige for Student Council President! Wait until I see Paige tomorrow!"

Alex slept very well, and dreamed heroic dreams about tomorrow.

Robert Healy

24. A bad day for bullies

The next day Paige rushed into homeroom to look for Alex. She waived him over to the door and, in hushed tones. She told Alex the mysterious vandal had struck again and ruined one of the posters.

"Look, this time they pasted the locker room picture of me in my underwear onto the campaign poster."

Paige's face turned red when she showed the vandalized poster to Alex.

"Where was the poster located, Paige?"

"The one on the bulletin board across from our lockers. And they taped this note on my locker door! It says more new 'pics' will be posted on Blahblah later today. Alex, what are we going to do?"

Alex grabbed his backpack and said, "Let's go, we have to work fast to stop that pic posting and any more wrecked posters. By the way, the 'Exposer' is Charlene Gump!"

"Charlene! Are you sure? How do you know?"

"Later. Follow me!"

Paige followed Alex out the door, down the hall towards their lockers and asked, "Where are we going? We have to go to class soon. I don't understand how we will find out who did this. Alex, please tell me what we are doing!"

As they rounded the corner and arrived at their lockers, Alex said, "Patience, you'll see what I've done in a minute."

Alex opened his locker door and plugged a cable into his Spy-Cam. Then Alex booted up his laptop and plugged the other end of the cable into his PC USB port. He clicked the Spy-Cam app and twelve videos downloaded them from the Spy-Cam device.

Paige said, "Alex, what on earth are you doing?"

The computer screen flickered and thumbnails of twelve frozen images of people appeared. Alex scanned them and clicked on the one with Charlene's face.

Paige gasped, "Oh my God, that's Charlene. She's in most of my classes, including gym class! What is she doing?"

Alex clicked on the play arrow and they watched as Charlene approached Paige's locker. She held a note, which she taped onto Paige's locker door. Charlene stepped away from Paige's locker and walked to the bulletin board. She pasted the locker room picture of Paige onto the campaign poster. Then she looked left and right several times and retreated down the hall.

"Why that little rat! There's no doubt Charlene is the miserable creep who has caused all the trouble. It's totally clear in the video," exclaimed Paige.

Alex removed the Spy-Cam, put it in his backpack and turned to Paige, "OK, let's find Charlene as fast as we can, and before she has time to do any more damage."

The bell for first period rang and students filled the hallway. Paige said, "I know exactly where she will be for first period class. Follow me!"

They climbed the stairwell, marched through a double door and down the hallway to room C207.

Paige looked into the classroom. "Good, she's not here yet, Alex."

Paige turned and spotted Charlene, the cyber-bully, coming in their direction. "Get ready Alex, here she comes."

"Oh hi Charlene," said Paige with a fake cheery smile. "Have a minute? There is something you have to see to believe."

Charlene looked perplexed and said, "Later, class is about to begin."

Paige put her arm out and said, "Oh Charlene dear, I think you would rather see this video before the principal does. Why don't you step over here and take a look? Like NOW!"

Charlene lost her confident appearance, but said, "Oh whatever," and stepped toward Paige.

Paige turned to Alex and said, "Please show darling Charlene what we think is so interesting."

Alex unzipped his backpack, pulled out his already booted laptop and brought up the Spy-Cam App.

Charlene impatiently said, "What is this nonsense? I have a class to attend. Why are you like wasting my time?"

Alex said, "Wasting your time? We'll see about that!"

He clicked the video arrow. They all watched as Charlene approached Paige's locker with the note and taped it to the locker door. They watched as she glued the picture to the poster and then she looked in both directions twice, retreated down the hall.

Charlene protested, "This video is so illegal. You have like totally violated my rights. You are both going to be in real trouble for this. And it doesn't prove anything!"

Paige opened her backpack to show Charlene the note and the poster picture; "Oh I think there are some pretty good finger prints on this poster and on your note. And we have evidence that you are the cyber-bully, "The Exposer" as well. Between the video and the other evidence it will be an open and shut case for the police."

"Police. Who said anything about police? Hey it was just a prank. Let's not get carried away. Give me a break here."

"Why should I give you a break? You seemed to not care about what you were doing to me. Why did you do it anyway?"

"I'm so sick of you being Miss Perfect … with perfect grades, and all the boys looking at your perfect smile, your perfect clothes, of the 'oh, so too perfect' Paige Madison. And now you're probably going to beat me out of being Student Council President. I couldn't take it anymore. You had to be stopped."

"Charlene, I think you could have stopped right after you said, 'I'm so sick.' I feel sorry for you. You are such a loser. Well, I have the video, the poster, the note and the 'Exposer' evidence. I'll hold onto them, while I think about what to do next. Meanwhile if you ever post anything about me on my locker, on Blahblah or anywhere, you will be so totally busted. And I'm talking about a police complaint! Am I clear?"

Charlene looked away from Paige and nodded her head yes.

"And I think you should drop out of the Student Council election today, while you're at it. You are not fit to be Class President."

Paige turned to Alex as Charlene slumped and sheepishly walked toward the door to classroom C207.

"Thanks Alex. I don't know how you thought up the Spy-Cam thing, but you are awesome. Thanks again and see you today at lunch maybe? We could go to Mega-Burger."

"Lunch? OK. Yeah, right lunch, for sure. See you."

Alex walked away feeling like a bona fide hero. He tripped over his feet, when he turned to look back down the hall at Paige. Paige smiled and waved.

Paige walked into her classroom thinking Alex was such a special guy after all, and kind of cute in a nerdy way. She started to plan exactly how their lunch would go.

Robert Healy

25. Payback at the park

Alex came home from school feeling like a super-hero, well at least way-swag. He was the man. He had busted Charlene, so Paige thought he was Superman. Lunch with Paige was awesome and life was so good! He ran upstairs two steps at a time to tell Buddy the good news and thank him for identifying "The Exposer."

Alex grabbed the leash and took Buddy for their walk to the park. Alex babbled all the way. He retold how the Spy-Cam video had busted Charlene, and how Paige thought he was so awesome, and how they had lunch together and blah, blah, blah. When they arrived at the park, Alex took Buddy off-leash, so they could play fetch with a tennis ball. Alex threw the ball as far as he could with a high arcing toss. Buddy raced at top speed, leaped, stretched his head forward and caught the ball in mid-air, on the first bounce. Alex marveled at Buddy's athleticism. He was so fast and so agile. People were so clumsy compared to animals. Buddy trotted back with the ball toward Alex. Buddy dropped the ball, looked behind Alex, lowered his head and growled.

Alex reached out, rubbed Buddy's head and said, "What is it Buddy?"

A familiar voice answered, "It's your worst nightmare you little nerd!"

Alex recognized Bart's gnarly voice. He spun around so quickly, that he almost fell down. Bart stood before him, bigger, stronger, meaner, and with a twisted, angry scowl that would frighten a serial killer. Alex reflexively backed away. Bart took another step forward, getting in Alex's face. Alex retreated again.

"So Alex is the big shot hero for little Miss Perfect, Paige Madison. Well, you're going to regret making trouble for Charlene."

"Charlene? I didn't think you had a girlfriend. I mean I didn't know about you and Charlene."

"Charlene is my cousin you creep and you're going to pay for all the trouble you caused her."

"Wait a minute, Charlene started all this. She was the trouble maker."

"This isn't a debate Logan. I'm going to stomp the heck out of you. And when I'm finished Paige won't even recognize you."

Bart raised his fists and stepped forward to attack. Buddy bared his teeth and made a deep growl worthy of a wild animal. The hair on his back stood up, his ears flattened back, his fangs were exposed and his eyes locked onto the advancing Bart. Bart stopped, looked at Buddy and stepped back in fear, almost tripping. Buddy stepped forward and made even scarier guttural noises that sounded like he was a mad-dog.

Bart panicked and blurted, "Get the dog away from me or I'll call the police."

Alex reached down and held Buddy by the collar. Buddy tugged strongly against Alex's grip, while he continued to snarl and bare his teeth.

"OK. Now I think it's you who better get away from here Bart. I don't know how long I can hold Buddy off."

Bart turned and walked at a brisk pace away from Alex and Buddy and yelled over his shoulder, "This isn't over Alex. You won't always have your dog to protect you. You're going to be sorry you ever messed with Charlene and me!"

Alex and Buddy hurried back home and up to Alex's room.

"Alex, you were right! This Bart creep is bad news. What a thug!"

"See what I mean! Now he'll be after me even more than usual. Remember, the fight is never over until Bart wins! What am I going to do now?"

"Bart probably acts this way because he has been bullied too and he thinks it's the way to be. Or he could have more serious problems. I think it's a good idea to avoid this kid."

"I try, but he's always nearby at school. When he sees me, he often starts trouble. Everyone else watches, thinking poor Alex can't defend himself. But at the same time they're glad it's not them that Bart is tormenting!"

"Alex, when you grow bigger and stronger you'll find that Bart will pick on someone else. For now, go about your business and try not to make eye contact. But if he attacks you again, you must man-up and report him. You can't run away from bullies. That only encourages them to bully more. But make sure you have witnesses who will back you up."

Alex's phone beeped indicating he had received a new e-mail.

"For starters Alex, save this video. It might come in handy."

"What video?"

Alex checked his phone and saw a new e-mail message with an attachment. Alex opened the attachment and viewed the video. It showed Bart threatening Alex, raising his fists and moving toward him. Then he stepped back in alarm and threatened Alex again as he left.

"How did you do this Buddy? You are amazing!"

"It's all included in my 'secret spy-dog, best friends, premium service package.' I have a built-in spy-cam that captures audio and video. Comes in handy sometimes."

"I'll say. If Bart ever threatens to make a complaint about us, I'll show him this. After that, he won't dare make trouble."

"I told you I am better than your Spy Cam XL-15."

"Totally dude! Totally!"

Buddy texted Pepper to find out how she was doing.

"Pepper, what's new?"

"Another day, another rabbit. How about you?"

"My friend Alex needs a lot of advice, but life is pretty good here."

"We had to escape the NIA agents again, yesterday. I hope they get tired of looking for us soon and either move on to somewhere else or give up."

"Pepper, maybe you should think about getting adopted by a family like I did."

"The pack is my family now, and I like the freedom. Thanks anyway. See you around."

"Have it your way, but let me know if you need anything."

26. Gambling does not pay

Alex squirmed in his chair, next to his mom in the principal's office. Mr. Pealing glared with angry eyes locked onto Alex and then made eye contact with Mrs. Logan. He straightened a pile of papers on his desk, coughed and spoke in a low and grave voice.

"I'm sorry to tell you that your son Alex is in serious trouble. It has come to my attention that Alex has been running a gambling operation and several students have lost substantial sums of money to your son. Obviously, we cannot tolerate this kind of behavior."

"Alex, a gambling operation? You must be mistaken Mr. Pealing."

"We'll soon see. We set high standards here at Chester A. Arthur Middle School and we have a zero tolerance policy for this kind of behavior. I have not reported the incident to the authorities, because of Alex's age, but Alex must be properly punished. I am considering a suspension and of course, this incident will go on his permanent school record."

Mr. Pealing paused for effect and glanced over the top of glasses at a cowering Alex Logan.

"Any college that considers Alex for admission, should know what kind of character they are dealing with." Pealing paused again.

Mrs. Logan asked, "What kind of gambling are you talking about?"

Pealing, cleared his throat, looked directly at Alex and suggested, "Perhaps you should explain exactly what was involved, since you are the guilty party."

Alex squirmed again and looked at the carpet.

Mr. Pealing growled, "Well Alex, we're waiting."

Alex looked up meekly at his now angry and embarrassed mom. Principal Pealing sat stone-faced and peered at Alex over his glasses. Alex looked back down again at the carpet and began his confession in muffled tones.

"Well, it seemed like a fun idea at the time."

"A FUN idea?" Mr. Pealing's voice boomed. All the while, Pealing glared at Alex with bulging eyes.

"Well, sort of," squeaked Alex. "I mean, we did it to have some fun, that's all," Alex pleaded.

"I guess you're not having 'FUN' now Logan," said Mr. Pealing.

Pealing's eyes squinted and his lips pressed together, so they were a thin downward drooping line on his face. He slapped his desk with a thundering blow for emphasis. The impact of his hand caused papers to fly away and shook the 'Principal of the Year' plaque on the office wall behind him.

Alex jumped back in his chair and then slumped forward.

"Go on Alex, how did this gambling thing work?" his mom asked.

"It was pretty simple. We bet on baseball and I acted as the "House," which means everyone made their bets with me. Each person picked any three major league baseball players, on any given game day. If their three players had a combined total of five hits or more on that day, they won the bet."

Mr. Pealing stood up and said, "There, there you have it, he admits to this gambling scheme. I tell you we cannot accept this behavior!"

"Just a moment," said Mrs. Logan "I'd like to hear the rest of the story. Go on son."

"I love baseball, as you know. They have stats for everything, like, you know, RBI's, batting averages, ERA's, slugging percentages, everything imaginable."

Pealing interrupted Alex saying, "What does that have to do with anything?"

"Well, Mr. Pealing, I went on-line to this totally cool baseball statistics website. I determined who the top 30 major league hitters were last year. I downloaded all of their at-bat stats from last year's games and figured out how frequently three batters had five or more combined hits on any single day. It turned out that happens only about 33% of the time. That meant I should win the bets two times out of three. So I decided to use five or more hits as the bet. My friends have made bets with me for about a month and of course, I have been winning."

Then Alex swallowed hard and said, "There's not much else to say mom."

"If your father was here he would be shocked and ashamed of you young man."

Alex lowered his eyes in shame.

"How and where did you make these bets, son?"

"Usually by phone, text message or e-mail or when we stopped for a soda at Burrito Bell on the way home from school. That's where we settled the bets."

"What about here at school?"

"No, we never had to with texting and everything. Everyone has a cell phone or a tablet or something."

"So, if I understand you correctly, you never actually made or paid the bets here on school grounds. Is that correct?"

"Yes, no, I mean we never made the bets at school, mom. We didn't have to. And we settled all the bets at Burrito Bell. You can ask any of the kids. Honest!"

"Honest? Look, we are wasting time here. Alex has already admitted to gambling Mrs. Logan."

"Yes, Mr. Pealing, but I wanted Alex to have a chance to tell the whole story, so I could decide what kind of punishment to impose."

"Just a minute," Mr. Pealing barked, "Let's not forget about what kind of discipline Alex will receive from the school. And of course there is the matter of restitution for the students, who were his victims. For example, Bart Quisling, who had the courage to report Alex's gambling operation, says he lost $20!"

"Bart Quisling? Twenty dollars? He never even made a bet with me. I would never be dumb enough to make a bet with Bart! He's lying to get me in trouble."

"Look young man, you're the one in trouble here, not Bart. Now let's get back to what kind of consequences there will be for you!"

"I quite agree, but let's discuss the school's role for a moment. Mr. Pealing, you say gambling is prohibited by the school regulations?"

"Of course it is, Mrs. Logan! Gambling is against the law, isn't it?"

Mrs. Logan considered this and responded, "Well yes and no. It seems gambling is not illegal when you purchase State lottery tickets, or if you play bingo at church, buy a raffle ticket, or make a bet in a pool for the Super Bowl or the NCAA Basketball tournament. And let's not forget all the 'Native American' legalized casinos. Mr. Pealing have you ever told the students they could not gamble on the school grounds?"

"Well, not specifically, but isn't it obviously wrong Mrs. Logan?"

"You and I may think so, but I would not expect everyone would agree with that. I would not expect school kids to know for certain, without being told directly not to gamble. May I see the regulation prohibiting student gambling?"

"Well, I'm not sure gambling is specifically itemized in the regulations. What exactly are you suggesting Mrs. Logan, if I may ask?"

"Thank you for asking Mr. Pealing. I am in complete agreement with you that Alex should be punished for this incident. I do not wish Alex to cultivate the bad habit of gambling. I will certainly restrict some of his privileges for quite a while. And if you or Alex can provide a list of the students who lost money, I will have Alex return their bets."

"OK, now let's discuss the school's discipline in this matter," said Mr. Pealing.

"Please excuse me Mr. Pealing, but I'm not sure any action by the school is warranted in this case. Certainly not one that permanently blemishes Alex's school record."

"I'll be the judge of that Mrs. Logan," said Pealing.

Mrs. Logan looked respectfully at Mr. Pealing and said, "Mr. Pealing, apparently none of the alleged infractions took place on the school property. I think this fact places the issue beyond your area of responsibility. Secondly, since no specific policy against gambling exists nor had it been communicated to the students or the parents, it would be unfair to penalize Alex and blemish his school record. I suggest that rather than have an embarrassing public dispute over this issue, perhaps it would be best to have the well-meaning adults in this room, agree on reasonable disciplinary action and then leave it in my hands to resolve.

Pealing sputtered something; thought again and reluctantly nodded his agreement. He then added, "Let this be a lesson to you young man. And rest assured, I will be watching you closely from now on."

Alex bowed his head submissively, but also to hide a slight smile that formed.

Mrs. Logan expressed her gratitude to Mr. Pealing for bringing the matter to her attention. He muttered something about it being part of his job and being interested in the welfare of the children. With that, hands were shaken and they left.

In the car, Alex's Mom said, "Well you certainly out-did yourself this time young man. What have you to say for yourself?"

Alex squeaked out a pitiful, "I'm sorry Mom."

"You are grounded mister for two weeks and NO TV or video games either," barked his Mom.

"But Mom, we were just having fun, and besides, I should probably get some sort of math award or extra credit for figuring out all those batting statistics and betting odds."

"OK, here's your award, make it three weeks smarty!"

Alex smiled to himself, thinking how his mom was pretty awesome. She talked so smoothly with Mr. Pealing and made sure the meeting didn't get out of hand.

"And you'll have to pay back all those winnings, like the $20 to Bart."

"Mom, Bart never made a bet with me. He is getting back at me for busting his cousin Charlene, for defacing Paige's campaign posters. That's why he ratted me out to Pealing!"

"It's his word against yours, and right now your word doesn't look too good."

"You can't make me do it!"

"Yes, I can and it's not your call! Now I suggest you quit while you're behind!"

"I wish Dad was here. He'd understand. You just don't get it!"

Alex regretted what he said, and tried to take it back.

"I'm sorry mom. I didn't mean that."

His Mom said OK, but the look on her face revealed that the hurt was deeper and would last longer.

When they arrived home, Alex's Mom told him to go up to his room and finish his homework … "And no games or TV for three weeks!"

Buddy could see Alex was upset and texted, *"What's up pal?"*

Alex told the whole story about the baseball gambling, how Bart busted him and gets $20 too. Then he told Buddy about how he was nasty to his mother and now felt bad.

"I knew this gambling thing would be a problem. But, why were you nasty to your Mom?"

"Because I was angry about having to pay that thug Bart $20 for nothing!"

"What did you say?"

"Oh something like I wish Dad was here because he would understand and she doesn't. But I took it back right away."

"Words once said can't be taken back, because the harm is done."

"She said OK, but she didn't look OK."

"She said OK because she loves you, not because she isn't hurt. You know, you are not the only one who is sad and misses your Dad. I've heard her crying at night when you are asleep. Your Dad would expect you to support her every way you can. Just sayin."

"OK. I guess I have been a jerk. My bad!"

"Let's say you've been mega lame. Now go downstairs and give her a big hug. And tell her again you are sorry and that you love her!"

"Do you think she'll ever forgive me?"

"Moms are very good at forgiveness, Alex."

"Lucky for me!"

Next, Buddy sent a text to Pepper.

"Pepper, is everything alright?"

"No, not really, Buddy."

"What happened?"

"The runt, Marcel, wandered away last night. Not far, but far enough to be taken by coyotes. We heard him yelp, but nothing after that. We tried to find him to help, but he had disappeared, just gone! It all happened so fast."

"That's terrible. I'm so sorry to hear it. How's Molly taking it?"

"She's pretty broken up. You know how she feels responsible for everything."

"How about you, Pepper?"

"I'm hanging in there. It's part of what happens out here in the wild."

"Take care of yourself!"

"Don't worry Bro, I will."

Robert Healy

27. Pepper gets lonely

After lunch on Saturday Buddy texted Alex and they met in his room.

"Alex, Pepper wants to meet with me this afternoon."

"What for?"

"She's lonely and a little down about living in the wild. She misses me and wants to talk."

"So, what do you want to do?"

"She doesn't know how to get here, so I will go and meet her behind the Mall."

"Your plan sucks. Isn't that where you were captured before?"

"It's an OK place to meet because we won't stay there, we'll go somewhere else to talk."

"But my Mom will wonder where you are!"

"Right. That's why I need your help!"

"What do you want me to do?"

"Take me for a walk to the park this afternoon. I'll go off to meet with Pepper and come

back to the park afterward. You hang out there for a couple hours until I come back."

"The plan is totally bogus dude. It's like so not safe!"

"Do you have a better plan?"

"No! But your plan is so not smart!"

"Hey, I need your help on this?"

"No need to go all hyper on me. Of course I'll help you!"

At 12:45 PM Alex took Buddy's leash, grabbed a tennis ball and told his Mom he was taking Buddy to the park.

"Don't forget, you promised to mow the lawn today. It gets dark earlier now, so be back home no later than 4:30 PM OK?"

"OK Mom. No problem."

To save time, Alex rode his bike and held Buddy's leash as he trotted happily alongside. They arrived at the park in ten minutes and Alex let Buddy off the leash.

"Buddy, it's now 2:00 PM and I have to be back home by 4:30. So that means you have to be back here by 4:00 PM at the latest!"

"No sweat. I'm meeting Pepper at the Mall at 2:30 PM. We'll chat for an hour or so; you know to see what's on her mind. I'll be back here before 4:00 PM."

"OK. I'll hang out here chillaxing. But Buddy, be careful and don't be late!"

Buddy disappeared through the hedges.

Robert Healy

28. Taken again

Alex chilled at the park and listened to tunes on his smartphone. At 4:00 PM he started to get concerned because Buddy had not returned.

"Ding," Alex was about to text Buddy when his phone signaled he had a message. Alex thought, This is probably Buddy telling me he's on his way.

Alex looked at the message and nearly dropped his phone. He had a horrible sinking feeling inside, like his heart had stopped, and was somehow about to burst out of his chest.

The message from Buddy was disastrous. *"Novato Animal Control captured Pepper. She is locked in a cage on the truck. I'm sure he's taking her to NARC.. I'm going to follow the truck. Buddy."*

Alex read the message twice, but could not believe his eyes. He thought, I knew this was a bad idea. I never should have allowed Buddy to do it. This is my fault. What if Buddy gets caught? What will to happen to him and Pepper?

Alex texted, *"Buddy, wait. What are you doing?"*

Alex's mind raced with a flood of thoughts that were headed straight toward panic. Alex grabbed his bike to race home. He was not sure what to do next, but he thought, Mom always knows what to do!

"*Ding*," another message arrived. Alex pulled out his phone to check it out.

"*I was right. The truck pulled into the NARC parking lot. I need help!*"

"*Buddy, stay where you are. I'll have mom drive us there and pick you up. And we'll try to get Pepper too.*"

"*Ding*!" *Something's wrong. The dogcatcher and another guy are putting dogs in carry cages and loading them into a truck. I think Pepper is being dognapped with the others and they are being taken somewhere else! Better hurry! PS- I cc'd Sean Keegan, our lab tech friend to see if he can help.*

"*Ding*," *Alex, I'm on my way to NARC. Meet me there. Sean.*

Alex reacted, thinking, No time to go home now! Alex turned his bike around and pedaled furiously toward NARC, which was only ten minutes away, maybe less at the speed Alex was traveling.

Alex wheeled into the NARC parking lot and saw a car parked near the entrance. As he approached the car, the door opened and Sean Keegan emerged. Sean put his index finger to his lips in the universal "*SHUSH*" sign.

He whispered "Hi Alex, I'm Sean Keegan."

Alex also whispered, "I got here as fast as I could. What's happening? Where's Buddy?"

Sean gave Alex the "*SHUSH*" sign again, "The two men are at the loading bay on the side of the building. They are loading dogs into a truck. Buddy went to investigate. I think we should take a closer look."

Alex dropped his bike into the bushes and they snuck around the corner. They crouched low, stayed close to the building and shrubs, until they reached the truck, which had it's back door rolled up. Buddy poked his nose out from the bushes and joined them. The voices of the two men drifted out through the open doorway.

Sean whispered, "Let's see what's in the truck. We don't have much time. Alex, you stay here, out of sight!"

Sean climbed up the ramp into the truck and crawled toward the cages with Buddy right behind him. Alex disregarded Han's advice and followed him and Buddy into the truck. Sean heard Alex crawl into the truck close behind him. He jabbed his finger repeatedly, telling Alex to get out of the truck and back into the bushes. Alex turned to exit the truck as the two thugs reappeared through the doorway.

The dogcatcher was a big man with a shiny skinhead and a weird dark blue tattoo on his neck with geometric shapes. He took off his official dogcatcher jacket and tossed it through the window into the truck's cab. Underneath he wore a T-shirt that said, "Does not play well with others," and Alex didn't doubt that for an instant. Alex thought, No wonder these dogs are scared, he's the creepiest dude ever!

The dogcatcher's NARC partner came through the doorway right behind him. He was even sketchier looking. He must have been allergic to water, because his matted hair hadn't been washed or combed for what looked like years. There was a huge tattoo on his arm that said, "Don't Tread on Me," with a picture of a coiled snake. He had a scar on his face that ran from his right ear to the corner of his mouth. If the dogs were afraid of the big guy, they would be in total panic when they saw Scarface.

Sean, Alex and Buddy retreated into the shadows in the front of the truck, hoping to not be seen. The men hoisted a final cage into the truck and pushed it forward. Sunlight illuminated the cage briefly.

Alex whispered, "Hey, that dog looks like Buddy!"

"It must be his sister Pepper, Alex."

The big guy walked around to the driver's door. It made a rasping squeaking noise when he opened it and then slammed it closed making a hollow "*BONG*" sound. Scarface reached up, grabbed a strap and pulled the cargo door down with a hard thud shook the truck. There was a scraping metallic sound, as the door latch locked into place, sealing the captives inside in their mobile jail.

Scarface turned and accidentally kicked something in the grass. He bent down to examine the ground and yelled out, "Hey Elmer, this is my lucky day. I found somebody's smartphone, lying here in the grass. Finders keepers," and he slipped the phone in his pocket.

Alex grabbed at his pocket for his phone, and found it was empty.

"Oh no, my phone! It must have fallen out of my pocket when I climbed into the truck."

Alex now felt even guiltier because he had not listened to Sean, about not getting into the truck. "You stay here, out of sight," Sean had said!

"Sean, we need help!"

Sean cursed, "I left my phone in the car."

Alex looked at Buddy, but then he realized the only contact information Buddy had was for him, Sean, Dr. Gore, some ARI researchers and the NIA agents.

"Oh no! What are we going to do now?"

"We'll think of something," Sean said without any conviction.

The dogs barked loudly. Scarface said, "Shut up" as he slammed the truck's front door with another resonant "*BONG*". The engine turned over with a grinding, churning sound and then roared to life. The engine valves clattered and then quieted down.

When the engine returned to idle, Alex and Sean heard one of the men say, "Well good old Dr. Gore should be real happy with this bunch. Maybe he'll give us a bonus."

The truck lurched forward and gained speed. It made a few turns and the tire-hum became louder as their speed increased on the highway.

Sean whispered urgently to Alex, "Those two goons must be taking the dogs to Dr. Gore at the ARI research lab! Alex, we need a plan and quickly. ARI is only two exits away."

"What if we make a diversion when we get there, Sean?"

"Good idea, but what kind of diversion?"

"Suppose we let all the dogs out of their cages? When they open the truck door, the dogs will run free in every direction trying to get away. Maybe in the chaos, we'll have a chance to sneak away unnoticed with Buddy and Pepper."

"But what if some of the dogs are not friendly when we let them out of the cages? They are all scared to death, you know."

"It's a risk, Sean, but we know for sure that neither of those goons are friendly. What do we have to lose?"

"Right, Alex. Let's do it!"

Dim sunlight filtered into the truck, through a small dirty skylight in the ceiling. Buddy led Alex to the first cage. Alex unlocked the cage door, and the dog that looked like Buddy emerged. Alex realized this was Buddy's sister Pepper. One by one they unlocked all the other dog cages. The dogs all attacked Alex and Sean with slurps and kisses of appreciation.

The truck veered to the right, slowed and stopped at the end of an exit ramp. They turned right and began to climb a hill. The truck slowed and hopped over a speed bump. Several more bumps followed. The truck moved more slowly now on a patchy road that had some potholes. Soon the tires made the gravely sound of an unpaved driveway. The truck stopped abruptly. Some of the cages slid toward the front of the truck. One of the truck doors opened with a screech and then slammed shut. They heard a buzzer or bell ring loudly. Shortly afterward, there was a muffled conversation, they could not decipher. They heard a rumbling, creaking sound and the hum of an electric motor. It sounded like an overhead garage door being opened. The sound stopped and the truck moved slowly forward and then stopped again. They heard the same rumbling, creaking sound again and a loud "thump" as the door closed completely. They were certain the truck was parked inside some sort of a building garage, because of the resonating echo of the engine.

Two security guards approached the truck.

One said, "I'll have to call upstairs. Wait here."

The big goon responded, "Tell Dr. Gore his dogs are here."

The ring-tone from Alex's phone shouted out from Scarface's pocket. The call was from an increasingly desperate Mrs. Logan, trying to reach Alex. Scarface ignored the call and set the phone to silent, vibrate mode. He would worry about the phone later. Maybe he could get a finder's fee from the owner or better yet, sell it on Craig's List.

The guard phoned upstairs to advise Dr. Gore about the shipment of dogs, while the goons opened the rear truck door. Scarface unlocked the latch, raised the door and all of the dogs jumped out of the truck and ran around the loading area.

"What the heck! How did they get loose," yelled Scarface?

The big guy said, "Quick grab those cages and let's round up those dogs!"

Scarface leaped into the truck to grab some cages and he came face to face with Sean and Alex.

"Elmer, quick, over here! These two idiots in the truck set the dogs free!"

The guards and Elmer ran over to the truck and captured Alex and Sean.

"We'll take these two upstairs. Dr. Gore will know what to do with them."

Alex stood stunned as Bart Quisling emerged from the truck's cab.

Bart sneered at Alex in mock surprise and said, "Uncle Elmer, I know this little creep. His name is Alex Logan. He goes to my school. He's the jerk that messed up Charlene's chance to be the Student Council President."

"Oh yeah, well it looks like he's gonna get some payback now!"

The security guards held Alex and Sean while the two goons recaptured the dogs and placed them back into their carry cages. Alex and Sean were shoved into the freight elevator along with the dogs and taken to the laboratory on the second floor. One of the security guards phoned Dr. Gore to say there was a complication. Dr. Seymour Gore waited with his arms crossed and a scowl on his face. Alex and Sean looked down at the elevator floor in defeat and tried to figure out what to do next. Their first attempt at escape had failed so utterly.

Robert Healy

29. Welcome back home to ARI

The freight elevator hummed and shook to a halt on the second floor. The extra wide doors parted vertically, like a giant mouth opening. The ARI guards pushed Alex and Sean forward into the hallway that led to the main lab room and an unhappy Dr. Gore. The thugs set the elevator to the "wait" position. One at a time they loaded the dogs onto wheeled carts and rolled them to the lab. The security guards pushed Alex and Sean into the lab.

Dr. Gore could not believe his eyes when he saw Sean stumble through the doorway. Dr. Gore's look of surprise quickly turned to one of evil glee as he locked eyes with Sean.

"Well, well, if it isn't the PITA animal rights crusader, Sean Keegan. Welcome back to ARI. But you are going to be sorry you came back here Sean."

Gore's, words dripped with the viciousness of deadly cobra venom.

"And who is this child accomplice with you, Sean? Recruiting them a little young at PITA these days aren't you?"

"He's innocent Gore. Let him go. It's me you want."

"I'm afraid it might be a little late for that Sean, but we shall see."

Gore motioned the guards, to take Alex and Sean to the far corner of the lab, while Dr. Gore examined the first two dogs wheeled into the lab by the thugs.

"Oh my, look at what we have here. It's my two favorite missing iMutts, Buddy and Pepper. You have been such naughty dogs, running away like you did. You have caused me a lot of trouble, with people you don't want to have trouble with. Thanks to you two, they may shut down my research program. So, I'm afraid you may no longer be useful to me; unless perhaps that operation still has a chance of success. But if that fails, I'll have to dispose of you both, and believe me, that will be a pleasure!"

Buddy and Pepper pawed at their cages and shivered with fear, as Alex and Sean looked on as helpless captives.

Dr. Gore turned, looked at Bart and asked Elmer, "Who is this other child?"

"Oh, Dr. Gore, he's my nephew, Bart. I thought it would be interesting for him to meet you and see the lab."

"Not a very timely visit I'd say, under the circumstances."

"True, but Bart identified this kid as a classmate, named Alex Logan. And you don't have to worry about Bart, he won't say anything to anyone."

"I should hope not, because all our 'butts,' as you would say, depend on that!"

Bart interjected, "I couldn't care less what happens to this Logan creep or his miserable dog!"

Alex's phone vibrated in Scarface's pocket. He cursed, removed the phone, and looked at the screen.

"Whoa, another call from someone named Dana Logan." Scarface blurted out, "I found the phone on the ground at NARC. This Dana Logan person keeps calling. Hey, the kid's name is Alex Logan. This must be his phone and that's probably his mom looking for him!"

Elmer mumbled, "What a genius!"

Dr. Gore shouted, "Don't answer it. Just put the phone on the table, while we figure out what to do."

Gore held his chin in his hand and mumbled out loud, "Well this Logan kid knows Bart and therefore they can find you two geniuses. He pointed at Elmer and Scarface. And Sean knows me and also about our little dognapping operation. I don't think PITA would approve of my experiments, do you Sean? I can easily get rid of Buddy and Pepper, but that still leaves us with these two."

Scarface interrupted, "Look I have two strikes already. If I get busted by the cops again, I'll go to jail for life, and that's so not happening! We can make these two disappear for good, Dr. Gore. I have a fishing boat docked in San Rafael. We'll knock these two out and put them into canvas sacks. Then we'll wait until dark and throw them into my boat down below deck. Tomorrow morning, real early, Elmer and I will take them out through the Golden Gate into the Pacific Ocean for a one-way deep sea fishing trip. We'll weight them down and dump them overboard out near the Farallon Islands, where the Great White sharks hang out. They'll be shark breakfast and nobody will ever see them again or be any the wiser."

Bart taunted, "Looks like you and your mangy dog are going to be shark bait, Logan!"

Alex shrunk back into the corner not knowing what else to do. As he did, he noticed a fire alarm plate on the wall. Alex made two slow steps sideways toward the alarm. When it was within his reach, he pulled the handle down hard. An alarm horn sounded with a howling screech and red lights flashed throughout the building. Dr. Gore ran to a telephone and frantically dialed the head of security in the building. The security guard answered, "Yes Dr. Gore. How can I help you? Is there a problem?"

Gore shouted, "NO, no problems. It's a false alarm. SHUT OFF those alarms NOW!"

The guard fumbled on his console and after a few frantic minutes, he silenced the alarms.

Then Dr. Gore said, "Call the Fire Department and the Police. Tell them it was a false alarm and not to bother responding."

"Right, Dr. Gore!" replied the security guard.

A few minutes later the phone in the lab rang. Dr. Gore ripped the phone from its cradle, "What now!"

The security guard sheepishly told Dr. Gore that he called the firehouse, but they had already dispatched police and fire to ARI, in response to the alarm. And besides, they had to follow their procedure and could not ignore the alarm. The fire station is only ten minutes away, so they would arrive in a few minutes.

Gore slammed the phone down and screamed, "Quick, take those two clowns and these two dogs into the surgery room. There's a door on the far side of the supply room, at the back of this lab. And lock the doors!"

The guard grabbed Sean, who fought back. Scarface hit Sean on the back of the head with a small lab fire extinguisher. Sean slumped to the floor, unconscious. The thugs dragged Alex and Sean through a small storage room at the rear of the lab and into the surgery room beyond it. They had barely closed and locked the doors to the surgery and returned to the lab, when the elevator doors in the hallway opened. Four emergency responders stepped forward. Three were firemen, dressed in full fire fighting gear with boots, helmets and axes. The fourth man was a policeman in his standard uniform. An ARI security guard had escorted the group to the second floor lab.

The guard babbled, "I'm sorry Dr. Gore. I tried to tell them there was no problem, but they insisted on coming upstairs to inspect the area where the alarm went off."

The Fire Chief stepped forward and asked, "Who is in charge here?"

Dr. Gore stepped forward and said, "I am the Executive Director of the lab, sir. Thank you for your concern, but everything here is under control."

The fireman ignored Dr. Gore saying, "I'll be the judge of that." He ordered his two firemen to check the rest of the second floor for any problems. They hurried away, accompanied by the ARI security guard.

"Now which alarm was tripped?"

Dr. Gore pointed at the alarm box near the corner.

The fireman asked, "How did that happen?"

Dr. Gore averted the Fire Chief's eyes and said, "Well we brought in this new shipment of dogs for our research and perhaps one of the cages bumped the alarm accidentally."

The policemen pointed at Scarface, Elmer and Bart, "And who are these people?"

Gore responded, "Oh they're guests who are here for a private tour of the lab."

"A private tour on Saturday evening? Isn't that a bit odd?"

Dr. Gore swallowed nervously and his eyebrow twitched slightly. "Oh, no! We often do off-hour tours, so we don't disturb the researchers, who do their important work during the day." A little spittle formed at the corner of Dr. Gore's mouth and a bead of perspiration descended from the top of his forehead.

The policeman thought … They don't look like any VIP's to me.

The two firemen returned after inspecting the rooms on the other side of the building. They reported there were no issues or problems that they could see.

The Fire Chief took a slow walk around the main lab. He looked for anything out of the ordinary but saw nothing unusual. He turned, apparently satisfied, and walked toward the others.

Alex let Buddy and Pepper out of their cages. He was frantic to direct the firemen's attention to the surgery room. He pounded on the door and yelled, but the intervening storage room absorbed the noise and nobody in the lab could hear him. Alex could see the fire trucks parked in the front of the building through the small surgery room window that did not open. The trucks sat there quietly with their lights flashing as three firemen stood around talking. Alex flicked the storage room light switch on and off to attract attention.

The Fire Chief noticed the lights flashing on and off in the storage room at the rear of the lab.

"What's wrong with the lights in that room?"

Dr. Gore said, "Oh the fluorescent tubes need to be replaced. They flicker all the time. Should have been fixed by now."

The Chief pondered, nodded his head and said, "OK, let's go."

The Chief looked around the room one more time, and turned toward the lab exit door. Dr. Gore placed his hands in his pockets and relaxed for the first time since the firemen had arrived.

The flickering lights had failed to get the Chief to investigate, so Alex looked for another way to get their attention. He noticed a gas burner on one of the lab benches at the back of the room. Alex opened a drawer below it and found a butane lighter the researchers used to light the burner. It was the long kind that people use to light gas barbecue grills and fireplaces. Alex grabbed the lighter and tested it. A one-inch flame leaped out of the front of the wand. Alex clawed his way up onto a table. He reached upward and after three panicked pulls on the butane lighter's trigger, a flame flickered out of the end of the lighter. Alex held the flame directly under a sprinkler head above the lab table.

As the Fire Chief walked toward the waiting elevator in the hallway, the fire alarms shrieked, bright red alarm lights flashed and a deluge of water poured from the sprinklers overhead. The firemen raced back into the lab. The Fire Chief looked toward the doorway of the storage room, where the lights had flickered.

"What's in that room?" he demanded.

Dr. Gore said, "It's a storage room with another lab beyond, that's all."

"Open the door, NOW!"

"I'm sorry I don't have the key at the moment," Gore said lamely.

"OK boys, break it down! There's some kind of problem in there."

Gore eased himself toward the exit, but was detained by the policeman, who engaged him in conversation. A fireman broke the lock on the storage room and then on the surgery room door with his axe. Both doors sprung open on the second blow. Two firemen entered the room and saw Alex, dripping wet, standing on top of a lab table holding the butane lighter. Sean Keegan was sprawled on the floor, rubbing the back of his head as he slowly returned to consciousness. Two wet dogs sat quietly on the floor.

The deluge of water stopped because one of the firemen had reset the system. Sporadic drips of water continued to fall from the sprinklers. The lab, the storage room and the surgery were soaking wet. The firemen led the motley crew of people and two wet dogs from the surgery into the main lab room.

The moment Alex and Sean re-entered the main lab, Dr. Gore made loud accusations.

"Intruders, they are intruders in my lab. They don't belong here! They must be the ones that have caused all this trouble. I recognize that one!"

He pointed toward Sean. "He's one of those crazy, so-called animal rights activists from PITA. He has been arrested here before and charged with trying to steal dogs from this facility. I don't know who this other child is with him. I've never seen him before in my life. Officer, arrest them both! They are trespassers!"

Sean spoke up as the policeman approached him with handcuffs. "Wait a minute, they're the criminals, pointing to Gore and the two thugs. Those two stole these dogs from NARC and brought them here to sell to this Monster Dr. Gore. They are not here for a tour; they provide stolen dogs to Dr. Gore for his illegal experiments. We were investigating their illegal dognapping operation, when we became trapped in their truck. You'll find the truck downstairs in the loading bay. Just before you arrived, they planned to kill young Alex and me and dump us at sea tomorrow morning!"

"Officer, that's a ridiculous charge. This is an important Research Institute. We are studying ways to slow aging and extend people's lives. We are not in the habit of killing people and dumping them at sea, I assure you. This fellow, Sean Keegan, will say anything to avoid another arrest. Well, you're not getting away this time Keegan!"

Alex spoke up saying, "Wait a minute! Why did they hit Sean on the head and knock him out? And why did they lock us in that room over there, where you would not see us?" Alex answered his own question, "So you wouldn't discover what they are actually doing at this lab, that's why."

"Officer, they are the trespassers here. This is my lab. They have no right to be here. They are making up pathetic stories. Please arrest these trespassers without further ado."

The policeman said, "Look this is confusing. But the Doctor has a point. This is private property and you are both intruders. So we'll have to take you two downtown until we can sort the stories out."

There was a pause in conversation. Alex's phone vibrated on the nearby table.

"Hey, that's my phone!" Alex leaped to the table and picked it up. A message appeared saying he had a new text message from Buddy. Alex looked at Buddy, who nodded his head. Alex opened the message, which said, "This might help them sort it out. Click on the video link."

Alex opened the video and hit the play button. The recording showed the events prior to them being locked in the surgery room. The audio was clear enough to hear every word said by Dr. Gore, the thugs and Bart.

The policemen told Alex and Sean to come with him. "We don't have time for phone chats now."

"Wait. Wait. Look at this video! This proves they are lying and that Sean and I are innocent!"

Alex waved them over to the phone. He held it up, hit play and increased the speaker volume. Dr. Gore stood stunned, as he watched himself discuss the plan with Elmer and Scarface to get rid of both Sean and Alex. He turned pale as he listened to the thugs talk about their plan to dump the bodies at sea. Bart cringed when he heard himself cheer for Alex and his dog getting what they deserved. They all watched Scarface club Sean with the fire extinguisher.

Gore lamely blurted, "That video is a trick. I don't know how he did it, but it's not real, I tell you!"

The policeman responded, saying, "Sure, sure it is. Dr. Seymour Gore, you are under arrest. You have the right to remain silent. You have the right to an attorney …"

Dr. Gore's phone signaled that he had a text message. He pulled his iPhone from his pocket and looked at the text. The message was from Buddy, and said, "Busted by your own technology, sucker!"

Gore glared at the message and screamed, "The dogs did it. Don't you see, the dogs are behind all of this?"

One of the policemen gently grabbed Gore's shoulder and asked, "Did you say the dogs are behind all this?"

"The video! The dogs made the video! This is a trick! It's the dogs! Don't you see?"

The policeman spoke to comfort Dr. Gore in a soothing voice, "Now, now Dr. Gore, everything is going to be all right. Come along quietly with us to the station house, like a good fellow. You can tell us all about the dogs there."

The policeman asked his partner to make sure a psychiatrist would be at police HQ to evaluate Gore when they arrived. He took Alex's phone as evidence. As he put it in his pocket, the phone rang again. The policemen looked at the screen. It was a call from Alex's Mom, so he answered it.

Mrs. Logan yelled, "Hello, hello, is anybody there?" and sighed with relief when the policemen finally answered her call.

The policeman said, "This is Sargent Wright. Yes I have your son Alex's phone. We are at the Aging Research Institute and Alex is okay. He's a little wet but otherwise fine. No, no Mrs. Logan, he's not in any trouble. We have had a situation here at ARI, involving your son and his dog Buddy that we'll have to sort out at police headquarters. No, we don't know why he was here at the Institute. Yes, we can meet with you at police HQ in let's say 20 minutes. No, you don't need a lawyer, at least not now. It looks like your son and another fellow have discovered a dognapping ring, recovered a bunch of stolen animals and uncovered other illegal activities going on here at the Institute. I'd say your son is one brave little hero Mrs. Logan. Yes, of course you can speak with him now."

The policeman handed the phone to Alex, saying, "Remember, I'll need the phone back. It's evidence."

"Hi Mom," said Alex meekly with his shoulders slumped and his eyes firmly rooted to the floor tiles.

"Where have you been all this time young man? You've had me worried sick! Half the neighborhood is out looking for you! You are in so much trouble, young man. This time you are going to be grounded forever! For three forevers! You wait until I get you home from the police station, mister!"

The line went dead. It wasn't a dropped call, more like a dropped kid. Alex handed the phone back to the policeman, who gave Alex a knowing, sympathetic look. Three more policemen walked into the room. They had been called for back up. One of them said that a CSI team was on the way to collect evidence.

"OK let's get these three to the police station for questioning and take statements from these two witnesses."

30. Vanished

With all the confusion in the lab, nobody noticed that Buddy and Pepper had quietly left the Main Lab room. They trotted down the stairwell and exited unseen through the lobby doors, which had been left open by the firemen. The dogs took the same route away from ARI they had used on the night they had escaped. They ran down to the highway, headed north and disappeared into the densely forested open-space to rejoin the pack.

"I hate leaving Alex all alone. I hope he will be OK."

"Buddy, it looks to me like he knows how to handle himself pretty well."

"Yeah, but it doesn't feel right not to be there for him, you know?"

"Look Buddy we had to get out of there, before someone from ARI or NIA discovered us. Besides, it was my only chance to escape so I wouldn't be sent back to NARC. Who knows what would happen to me there!"

"You have a point there. And I'm your brother, so I'm here for you. But I'll have to get back home so Alex doesn't worry."

"Text him dude and go home in a day or two if that's what you want."

"What about you, Pepper? Do you plan to stay in the woods forever?"

"I don't know. I like the freedom out here, but the comforts of a home like yours might be nice. Now I live the life of an outlaw, always on the run. But I'm not sure if I can ever trust humans. Look at what happened with those thugs, who sold us back to that monster Dr. Gore!"

"Yeah Pepper. I hear you, but look at who came to save us, Alex and Sean. There are good people and bad ones. People are like dogs, you have to judge them one at a time based on what they do."

"But that's risky and it takes time, Buddy."

"Pepper, you can choose to live in the woods if you think taking a chance with people is too risky, but I don't think life out there will be much fun either. The kids say 'YOLO', which stands for 'You Only Live Once.' Assuming you don't take stupid risks, it's not a bad philosophy. But sooner or later you have to be willing to trust somebody."

"OK. Easy for you to say because you're all set. You were lucky with your family. But what if someone like Elmer, Scarface or Bart had adopted you? It's too risky to take the chance."

"I get that and I was lucky. But what about Sean?"

"For one thing, we don't know if Sean even wants a dog living with him."

"Are you kidding? Sean loves animals. If he knew you needed or wanted a home, he'd offer one in a sec. Do you want me to ask for you?"

"I'll think about it, Buddy."

"OK but I'm heading back home tomorrow one way or the other." Buddy sent a text to Alex to that effect.

They came to a small clearing. Molly trotted toward them with her tail wagging, like a high-speed windshield wiper. Buddy and Pepper had hours of stories to tell the pack about their latest big adventure. Molly barked with joy and jumped into the air. She was thrilled to hear about Dr. Gore's arrest and the possible demise of his lab.

Robert Healy

31. Mom, meet me at the Police Station

Three squad cars pulled to the curb in front of Police Headquarters. Two policemen got out of the front seats of each car and opened the rear doors for their passengers. Three more policemen came out of the front door of the station to meet them. Bart and his uncle Elmer were in the first car. Scarface and Dr. Gore exited from the second car. Sean and Alex stepped out of the third. A medic met Sean, examined his head wound and gave him a cold pack, to hold against the growing bump on his head.

One of the policemen met with a man in a suit and pointed him toward Dr. Gore. The policeman nodded toward Gore, and twirled his index finger next to his temple, the universal sign for he's a little crazy. They were taken to separate rooms; the goons, Bart and Dr. Gore for interrogations, Alex and Sean to make witness statements. Dr. Gore screamed he wanted a lawyer all the way down the hallway. Elmer and Scarface were familiar with being arrested, so they quietly followed the police officer. They schemed together about how they could blame Dr. Gore for everything.

The moment Alex entered the police station; his Mom rushed over and embraced him with tears streaming down her face.

"Oh Alex, Alex, are you all right baby? I'm so glad to see you! Are you sure you're all right?"

"Oh Mom, don't go all emo on me. I'm fine."

"Alex, I'll go 'All emo' if I want to. I have been so worried about you!"

Alex thought … Maybe being grounded for three forevers, might become only one or two forevers.

One of the policemen interjected, "I'm sorry ma'am, but you'll have to wait here while they take Alex's statement. He won't be too long. Have a seat here, please."

"Don't Ma'am me. I'm going with Alex for God's sake! After what he has been through today!"

"I'm sorry, Mrs. Logan, but you must wait here for now. Don't worry; Alex is not the one in trouble. We need him to tell us what happened. If it gets any more complicated, I'll come back for you, so you can act as his guardian, OK?"

Mrs. Logan sat reluctantly and watched, as Alex disappeared into one of the rooms along the hallway, with a tall detective right behind him. Alex was directed to a chair as the detective and his partner took their seats across the table. Alex had rehearsed the story that he and Sean had worked out together at the lab, before leaving for the police station. They knew they would be asked to describe what happened, but in separate interviews.

The detective asked Alex if he would like something to drink and maybe a snack. A starving Alex said he would love something to eat, like a trail-mix bar and either a Gatorade or an Izze, if they had that. The detective said no problem and sent his assistant to fetch whatever he could find. While they waited, the detective asked Alex about school and other small talk. When the assistant returned with a Gatorade and two fruit and nut bars, the interview took a more serious turn.

Alex told them about going to NARC, hoping to find his lost dog. He met Sean Keegan in the parking lot. Sean was investigating the dognapping operation for PITA. Sean watched the NARC building on weekends, trying to catch the criminals in the act. They saw two men loading caged dogs into a truck. When he and Sean examined the truck, they found it was filled with caged dogs. They climbed into the truck to look more closely, but became trapped when one of the goons closed the truck's rear door. Alex told the policemen everything that had happened, while they were prisoners at ARI. How the criminals planned to dump them at sea; how he had set off the fire alarms, had blinked the lights and finally, set off the sprinklers to get the firemen's attention. The detective and his assistant wrote notes about everything Alex said. A tape recorder sat in the middle of the table and made Alex nervous. He felt a bead of sweat form because he couldn't make a mistake telling his story to the detective.

The detective sighed, put down his pen, looked straight at Alex and said, "There's one thing that troubles me. This video bothers me. How were you able to shoot the video while all this other stuff was going on?"

Alex felt a flash of panic, but he and Sean had anticipated the question. Together, they decided Alex would answer that question and Sean would simply say, "You'll have to ask Alex about that."

"I saw Dr. Gore take my phone from Scarface and put it on the lab table. I could see the situation was becoming dangerous for Sean and me. I thought someone has to be able to know what really happened here. While they were arguing among themselves about what to do with us, I snuck over and activated the camera in video mode, hoping it would help smart guys like you to solve the crime."

The detective and his assistant glanced at each other and nodded, accepting the "smart guys like you" part of the testimony, as highly believable.

"But it all seems so improbable, Alex. I mean, how you would be able to do that, without them noticing and stopping you."

"Well, I didn't say it was easy. Look at the video. It speaks for itself. It's all the proof you need. Or would you rather believe Dr. Gore's claim that the dogs did it! Just sayin."

Both officers laughed and closed their notebooks.

"I think that about does it, Alex. Thanks for your help. You are quite a brave and clever young man! We'll have to talk again and you will be a star witness at the trial."

Alex gulped the last of his Gatorade and almost ran from the room. He rushed down the hallway to his Mom, when cameras flashed, two men held TV cameras with bright lights and several reporters with microphones scrambled toward him.

The detective interceded, held up his hand and said, "Please let this young man have time alone with his Mom. He has been through a lot today."

The press ignored the detective and shouted more questions in rapid fire.

"When did you learn the dogs were being stolen from NARC?"

"How did you find out that Dr. Gore was doing illegal animal experiments at ARI?"

"Is it true they planned to kill you and Sean and dump you at sea?"

"How did you think to set off the fire sprinklers?"

"Did you think you were going to die?"

"How did you feel now that it's over?"

"How did you have the presence of mind to record the video?"

"How does it feel to be a hero?"

Alex's Mom stepped forward and said, "I'm sorry, Alex will not be answering any questions tonight. Please give us a break. There will be time tomorrow or the day after for comments."

The press groaned their disapproval at Mrs. Logan's suggestion and pressed forward again. They were about to re-launch their barrage of questions, when Bart, his father and their attorney, emerged into the hallway from an interrogation room. They strode briskly toward the front exit, with their heads down.

Someone yelled, "There's Trent Quisling and his son Bart!"

The reporters spun on their heels and rushed down the hall toward their new victims. The detective snuck Alex and Mrs. Logan out the side door unnoticed, while all this was happening. They hurried over to Mrs. Logan's car and sped directly home.

Alex's Mom asked questions all the way home. She sounded like the reporters and the detectives combined. She wanted to know everything imaginable. Alex stuck to the story he had told the detectives. After they pulled into their garage and parked, Alex's Mom reached over and gave him a huge hug.

"Alex, I was so worried and upset about you. I love you so much. And I'm so proud of the way you handled yourself. You could have been killed, but you kept your wits. Your father would have been so proud of you too."

"Thanks. I love you too and I'm so glad to be home."

"Speaking of home, Alex, where is Buddy?"

"After we were all safe and everything, he and his sister Pepper escaped into the woods. He'll come home tomorrow, I think."

"How do you know that? And how do you know Buddy has a sister?"

"OOPS!" Alex thought quickly and said, "Sean used to work at the lab and had recognized Buddy and his sister Pepper as the two dogs he had set free from the lab not long ago. The dogs had run off to live in the wild. But Buddy was captured, brought to NARC and then we adopted him. His sister still lives in the wild, I guess. It's sort of an epic story."

"But what if Buddy doesn't come home?"

"He will come home Mom. We're his crew now. Trust me, I know Buddy."

"OK. We'll see what happens tomorrow. Meanwhile Mr. Local Hero, would you like a brownie and some ice cream?"

"That would be totally sweet! I'm starved!"

Alex now believed he would be grounded for zero forevers.

Robert Healy

32. There's no place like home

Alex didn't sleep well that night. He was amped-up about the events of the day, but worried about Buddy, where he might be and if he was all right. He checked his laptop and saw a message from Buddy saying he was with Pepper and planned to return home in a day or two. Well, at least they had escaped safely, and for the moment had evaded the ARI guards and NIA agents.

In the morning, Alex bounded downstairs for some breakfast. Mrs. Logan was on the phone in the kitchen, trying to get rid of another reporter who wanted to interview Alex.

Later in the morning she talked to two TV networks that wanted exclusive interviews with the whole family. Mrs. Logan said she would consider their offers. Another person called about some sort of a magazine article. It was all simply crazy. The local news stations called Alex a hero and a boy techno-genius. The press van in front of the house drove the neighbors crazy. The van had a satellite dish mounted on the roof to transmit the reporter's story. One neighbor, that hardly knew Alex, was giving a TV interview.

She smiled and said, "I always knew Alex was an exceptional child, destined to do great things."

She was the one who had previously yelled at Alex and threatened to call the police if he stepped onto her lawn to retrieve a ball.

After lunch, Alex was on his bed. He heard the pet door slap. Probably the wind Alex thought, but it reminded him Buddy was out there somewhere in the woods. He thought about Buddy and wondered if he was okay. A few seconds later, Alex heard familiar rhythmic footsteps running up the stairs. Buddy jumped up onto the bed and knocked Alex backward. He licked Alex's face as Alex hugged him. Buddy's tail wagged wildly. Alex was so happy that he cried for joy. Buddy was back! He had sneaked through the back yard, unnoticed by the press.

Alex asked if Pepper was OK. Buddy nodded his head and then gave Alex a big wet kiss.

Alex wiped his tears and said, "Buddy, we love you so much!"

Alex had booted his computer so Buddy could use Bluetooth or WIFI to text him. This was because his cell phone was still held at Police Headquarters as evidence.

Buddy sent a text message, *Pepper and I had to get away in case the NIA agents looked for us when they arrived at the lab to investigate the events. I was worried they would find us.*

"No worries Buddy. NIA has bigger issues to worry about now, with Dr. Gore arrested and the reporters hounding them about animal cruelty."

Savannah came into Alex's room after she heard all the commotion. There were more tears of joy, as life tried to return to normal.

At 3pm, the doorbell rang. Mrs. Logan answered it, and expected to turn away another reporter. She was surprised when she saw who it was and went upstairs to Alex's room.

"Alex, there's someone special to see you downstairs."

Alex slumped downstairs wondering, What now?

Paige Madison stood in the foyer with her dog, Muffin. Alex invited Paige in and they walked to the family room and sat down. Buddy ambled over and sniffed Muffin. Muffin looked the other way, as if completely uninterested.

Alex noticed and thought, Don't worry Buddy, that's the way Paige treated me in the beginning. Maybe I should tell Buddy to be himself and not to show too much interest.

Paige said, "Alex, I'm here to thank you, again."

"Thank me? Thank me for what?"

"My dog Muffin wandered away on Saturday, like Buddy. We looked everywhere, but couldn't find her. That's because an animal control officer had captured Muffin and taken her to NARC. She has an identification chip in her ear, but because it was after NARC's regular hours and a weekend, NARC would not have notified us until Monday. But that would have been too late because Muffin was in that truck with you and the other dogs! Those thugs delivered her to that horrible Dr. Gore! Alex, you saved Muffin's life!" Paige wiped a few tears of appreciation from her cheek.

Alex said something dumb like, "Well, I didn't do that much. Anyone would have done the same thing."

"But it wasn't anyone Alex, it was YOU who saved Muffin and the other dogs! This makes two times you have been totally there for me."

Alex didn't know where this conversation was going, but he sure liked the drift.

Paige continued, "I am so hoping we can be really good friends Alex."

Alex almost choked and managed to squeak out, "Me too."

Paige smiled her radiant toothpaste ad smile as Alex blushed and looked away.

"Alex, would it be OK for me to stay a while? Maybe we can do some homework together."

Hearing that, Alex's Mom thought, What a good idea that was, and what a great girl, who will keep Alex focused on his schoolwork.

Then Paige said, "And if you want to take a break later, I'm pretty good at video games. I'm an ace at Dark Star Warrior - The Rebellion, if you have that game."

Alex said, "Are you kidding? Have it. I'm up to level six."

Paige responded, "Hey that's pretty great, you're only one level behind me."

Alex could not believe his ears. "So Paige, you like video games?"

"Love them. I beat my brothers all the time. I hope you won't mind losing to a girl sometimes, Alex."

"We'll see about that. You're a big talker, but I'm the iceman in all these games."

That was when it occurred to Alex that Paige Madison might be the coolest girl in the whole world.

Their wonderful conversation was interrupted, when the doorbell rang. Two big men in suits stood on the front porch. They had just parked their black Cadillac Escalade in front of the house. Mrs. Logan let them in. Alex noticed that Buddy slipped out through the pet door and disappeared under the deck. Deputy Les Smart and Agent Mason Dixon introduced themselves to Mrs. Logan and asked to talk to Alex. They said they had a few questions to clear up and it would not take long.

Alex told them about the whole series of events. The agents were particularly interested in Pepper and what Alex knew about her. Alex told them he had never seen that dog before but she was one of the dogs kidnapped from the NARC facility. They asked Alex what had happened to his dog last night. He told them that in the confusion, his dog had run away with another stray, but had found his way back home today.

Deputy Les Smart looked at Muffin, made eye contact with Paige (who he mistook as Alex's sister, Savannah) and asked, "And is this your dog?"

Paige responded, "Yes, yes it is."

Deputy Les Smart stood up, turned to agent Dixon and said, "That dog isn't anything like the description of the missing laboratory dogs. This was a waste of time. Now get your men back to the open-space and find those dogs before they get two counties away."

Deputy Les Smart turned to Alex's Mom, thanked her for giving them time, and told her Alex was a brave young man. They left in a hurry. The NIA agents were gone only two minutes when Buddy reappeared.

"What was that all about," asked Paige?

"Oh, nothing important. They seem to be looking for another dog that is missing, that's all."

Buddy gave Alex a wink. Alex saw it and smiled. He turned back to Paige and said, "OK. I'm ready if you are!"

"Oh yeah, the homework. What subject shall we work on first?" asked Paige.

"No, not the homework. I was thinking about us playing Dark Star Warrior!"

"Not until we finish our homework," said Paige.

Hearing that, Mrs. Logan smiled and returned to the kitchen.

33. The final chapter

One week later, Alex was still the Big Man on Campus at Chester A. Arthur Middle School. Even Mr. Pealing decided that Alex was a hero. Suddenly all the girls who previously would not give him the time of day chatted with him as he walked down the hallway. They laughed at his jokes and openly flirted. Alex made it clear that only one girl had his interest at the moment and she was Paige Madison. That seemed to make some of the girls even more interested in Alex.

Nobody had seen Bart Quisling for a week. His rich father had brokered a deal with the authorities for Bart to be a witness for the prosecution. In return, as a minor, he would not be charged with any crimes and he would be released on probation. Mr. Quisling agreed to have Bart undergo an behavioral counseling program and to report monthly to a social services caseworker for one year. In return, Bart would have no permanent arrest record.

A few students told Alex that Bart had withdrawn from Chester A. Arthur and had transferred to a military academy somewhere in Indiana that specialized in "problem children." Alex breathed a sigh of relief because Bart would not be around to harass him any more. It was rumored that the Quisling family had decided to move to another town, because of the social embarrassment caused by Bart's arrest with his Uncle Elmer.

Alex and his Mom watched a news interview with Mr. Gnarly, the spokesman for NIA, on the evening news. Mr. Gnarly said, "NIA had no knowledge of or involvement in illegal animal experiments. Dr. Gore was an employee of ARI, not NIA, so they were not responsible for his actions. NIA was appalled at Dr. Gore's alleged illegal and unethical activities. If the charges proved to be true, they hoped justice would be swift and harsh."

The evening of Dr. Gore's arrest, all of the ARI laboratory equipment and animals had mysteriously been removed, in the middle of the night. They were packed into unmarked trucks and shipped to an unknown warehouse for storage. The entire lab had been wiped clean with strong chemicals. The police were unable to find any clues about who was responsible, or determine where the equipment had gone. They found an unconscious police guard at the site, who only remembered being shot with a dart by an unknown assailant.

Buddy texted Sean about adopting Pepper. Sean was willing, but unable to, because dogs were not allowed in his apartment complex. Alex told his Mom the dire situation of Buddy's sister Pepper, living in the woods.

His Mom pondered quietly. She shocked Alex when she said, "Well I guess we have room for two dogs, don't you think?"

Buddy texted Pepper to meet him tomorrow morning at the cement storm pipe that went under highway 101, if she wanted to live with the Logan family. Pepper texted back that she would to give it a try, but made no long-term promises.

In the morning, Buddy made a final trip to meet Pepper and bring her back to the Logan house. This time Buddy kept a sharp eye out for dogcatchers. Being captured twice was enough! Pepper trotted through the storm pipe, when she saw her brother. They wasted no time and scampered back to Alex's house. There was a good chance Pepper would become part of the Logan clan. When they arrived home, Pepper and Buddy raced around the house, inside and out. Alex's Mom gave Pepper her first decent meal in many weeks, lamb and rice kibble with a little ground beef mixed in and a sprinkle of chicken broth. The food disappeared so fast that Pepper had redefined the meaning of the phrase "Wolfing down a meal."

That evening Alex sauntered upstairs with a smile on his face. He changed into his pajamas and jumped into bed. Buddy and Pepper jumped up as well. Alex lay there and thought about the events of the last couple of days, while he scratched Buddy's ear. Buddy was back home safe and sound. Pepper was no longer in the wild, and maybe would become a permanent member of Logan family. Bart would never bother him again. Paige and he were the best of friends. He was "The big man on campus," at least for a while. Alex wondered if life could possibly be any better, as he, Buddy and Pepper fell soundly asleep.

The End.

ABOUT THE AUTHOR

Robert Healy is a retired software marketing executive. He has written a book of Haiku poetry, "*In a Single Breath*", and an early reader book of Fairy Tales, "*Ysabel's Bedtime Stories*." Alex and the iMutts is his first novel. A second adventure novel is near completion. He has also written three show scripts performed in Marin County, CA. "*Sea to Shining Sea*," was a humorous short play. "*Winter Tales*," was a narrative with a compilation of holiday stories and poems from the 1600's to the current day. His most recent show script, "*The Gathering*," was a compilation of Irish humor and proverbs.
Bob lives in Northern California with his wife, Dana, their rescue dog, Kobe and their cat, Muffin.

Made in the USA
San Bernardino, CA
19 December 2014